GRABILL MISSIONARY
CHURCH LIBRARY

GOLD RUSH
PRODIGAL

★ ★ ★

BROCK & BODIE THOENE

GOLD RUSH PRODIGAL

★ ★ ★

BROCK & BODIE THOENE

BETHANY HOUSE PUBLISHERS
MINNEAPOLIS, MINNESOTA 55438

Manuscript edited by Penelope J. Stokes.

Cover illustration by Dan Thornberg,
Bethany House Publishers staff artist.

Copyright © 1991
Brock and Bodie Thoene
All Rights Reserved

Published by Bethany House Publishers
A Ministry of Bethany Fellowship, Inc.
6820 Auto Club Road, Minneapolis, Minnesota 55438

Printed in the United States of America

Library of Congress Cataloging-in-Publication Data

Thoene, Brock, 1952–
    Gold Rush Prodigal / Brock and Bodie Thoene.
        p. cm. — (Saga of the Sierras)

    1. California—History—1846–1850—Fiction. I. Thoene, Bodie,
1951–   . II. Title. III. Series: Thoene, Brock, 1952–   Saga
of the Sierras.
PS3570.H463G65   1991
813'.54—dc20   90–23617
ISBN 1–55661–162–5   CIP

In memory of
Shelly Nielsen
and Brian Wilson,
two of Glennville's own
who are Home.
Ora loa ia Iesu . . .

Books by Brock and Bodie Thoene

The Zion Covenant

Vienna Prelude
Prague Counterpoint
Munich Signature
Jerusalem Interlude

The Zion Chronicles

The Gates of Zion
A Daughter of Zion
The Return to Zion
A Light in Zion
The Key to Zion

Saga of the Sierras

The Man From Shadow Ridge
Riders of the Silver Rim
Gold Rush Prodigal

Non-Fiction

Protecting Your Income and Your Family's Future

BROCK AND BODIE THOENE have combined their skills to become a prolific writing team. Bodie's award-winning writing of the Zion Chronicles and the Zion Covenant series is supported by Brock's careful research and development. Co-authors of Saga of the Sierras, this husband and wife team has spent years researching the history and the drama of the Old West.

Their work has been acclaimed by men such as John Wayne and Louis L'Amour. With their children, Brock and Bodie live on a ranch in the Sierras, giving first-hand authenticity to settings and descriptions in this frontier series.

CHAPTER 1

William David Bollin stood on the deck of the schooner *Wanderer*. Ten days out of Honolulu and bound for Panama, his ship lay becalmed like the whaler across the way, whose roaring night fires were the beacon of her trade. The two ships had drifted within sight of each other just at sundown and had not as yet acknowledged each other's presence.

The orange fires leaping beneath the whaling ship's try pots threw gleaming streaks across the swells. In the moonless night the reflections of the twin blazes reached out and withdrew, then stretched toward the *Wanderer* again. To Bollin the light seemed like a forked spear probing for the heart of the ship on which he stood.

Even in the gloomy darkness of midnight, the contrast between the two vessels was evident. The *Wanderer* lay silent, waiting. Only a few of her crew were awake on this watch, hoping for a rising breeze that would fill the sails and carry them southeastward. The decks of the unknown whaler bustled with activity. The flames beneath the huge cast-iron pots made a rushing, crackling sound that carried clearly over to where Bollin leaned on the rail. Above the roar could be heard the rattle of chains and the dull clank of metal on metal. Punctuating the mechanical noise was the occasional muffled shout of some order being delivered.

The same sinister orange glow that reached out toward David Bollin also illuminated the deck and lower rigging of the whaler. Against this gleam the distorted shapes of men moved, grotesquely elongated and seeming to leap from canvas to canvas.

Unbidden, an image leaped to David's mind from the recesses of his childhood—a picture of hell, bathed in red sulphurous light, with figures of the condemned writhing in eternal pain. He shuddered inadvertently and glanced over his shoulder, then, angry with himself, consciously squared his shoulders and tightened his jaw muscles. His father would have seen the same vision of demons and hellfire, but he would have made it an image for his next sermon.

The thought of his father broke the eerie spell of the night. David shook his head in derision as he considered his father's life and work—twenty-five years pastoring a church in backwater Kohala, with only an occasional invitation to preach in the great Kewaiahao stone edifice in Honolulu. He had buried a wife, three children, and most of his life in the Hawaiian Islands. It didn't seem like much to show for twenty-five years.

Back down in his cabin, staring moodily into the dark rafters, David thought again how his father had hoped— no, *expected* him to follow in his footsteps. "Not likely," he muttered aloud. Even the disquieting spectacle of the whaler had more allure than the prospect of living and dying in some village, preaching to an all native congregation in exchange for a cramped house and second-hand clothing sent in barrels from far-off New England.

David's resistance to his father's expectation had made him jump at the opportunity for this sea voyage.

The death of his maternal grandfather back in Boston had made it possible. The old man had willed a substantial sum of money to David directly, perhaps harboring a grudge against David's father for his daughter's death ten years earlier.

The news of the windfall inheritance had been accompanied by a letter of credit. David also received the promise of a high-placed introduction to Boston society if he should "return to civilization."

He could still see his father's face reflecting deep disappointment and sorrow as David had made it clear that he would invest none of *his* money and no more of *his* life in Hawaii. David now shook his head in angry self-righteousness. How could his father have expected him to stay on when the means were present for him to escape?

Since the *Wanderer* had been in port at the time, booking passage for the Isthmus of Panama was a simple matter. Once there, a short overland trek would take David to another sailing vessel headed for Boston.

His letter of credit easily secured him first-class accommodations and much forelock-pulling by the officers and crew. Settling down to sleep, David's thoughts drifted back to the whaler still clanking and roaring nearby. David had once considered escaping the islands by signing on such a ship. He'd heard stories about how rough the life was, and now he was glad he'd waited.

David idly wondered if any of the whaling men now working through the night had ever been in Honolulu. Probably they had—drinking and carousing and pitching rocks through church windows. David's father had often used whalers as the perfect example of what drink and lawlessness could produce in men. David smiled to himself as slumber crept over him; he need not choose between the life of his father and the life of the whaling men. He would be a gentleman, a man of means.

It was still dark outside the mission house. Pastor William Bollin sat on the edge of his bed and looked impatiently out the window toward the west. Earth and sea and sky blended together in deep lavender hues still flecked with stars.

By now the sun would be bright over the ship that had carried David away. The thought made Pastor Bollin close his eyes, imagining his son bathed in sunlight on the deck of the schooner *Wanderer*. David would not be looking back toward Hawaii. William Bollin was certain of that.

The thought tied a knot of grief around his heart, making it difficult to breathe. He shook his head and opened his eyes, defying the waves of sorrow and the anger that threatened to drown him.

He looked down at the pages of his open Bible. The letters were too dark to read, and yet he knew them by heart. He spoke the words in the soft language of the people of Hawaii.

"Pomaikai ka poe e u ana." Blessed are those who mourn, for they shall be comforted. . . .

For twenty-five years, William Bollin had proclaimed those words; lived and walked in that truth through the death of a wife, two sons and an infant daughter. In the end, only David had been left to him. Now David was gone, and for the first time William found no comfort. Once again he murmured the prayer, the plea, that the hurt would fade and dissipate like the clouds that clung to the towering *palis* of the island he called home.

To his small native congregation, Pastor Bollin was known as *Kapono*—The Righteous. His son, called Kawika to his face, had earned the whispered name, *A'a*—Rough Lava. Just as lava cuts the feet of the traveler, young David cut the heart of his good father.

The saying was true, and yet nothing had cut so deep as this final parting of father and son. Days and nights had passed, but the grief had not diminished for Kapono Bollin. The people saw it clearly in the eyes of their beloved teacher, and their pity somehow made it more difficult for him to hide the ache.

Kapono Bollin had learned another side of the story of the Prodigal. The father had mourned for his son and had not been comforted.

———

When David awoke the next morning, he could tell that the *Wanderer* was still becalmed. He started up on deck, but checked himself and forced his feet into the unaccustomed pair of shoes. A gentlemen never went barefoot.

No breeze was stirring, but the captain cocked an eye at the horizon and ventured the opinion that they would see a change soon.

The whaler still lay off in the same position relative to the *Wanderer*, and the activity on its deck continued. David made his way to the spot on the stern where he had watched the previous night, and again he leaned on the rail. In the clear morning air he could make out the forms of two men with long poles warding off sharks from a huge strip of blubber being hoisted on board. Of the whale, little remained but a carcass, except for its gigantic broad head.

The fires of the try pots didn't gleam as brightly by day, but their baleful glare was replaced by an oily column of thick smoke. The smoke rose in a perfectly vertical shaft like a fourth mast, only much taller and blacker than the others. It ascended over the whaler until it reached a certain level in the air, then began to spread out in a layer of haze. The whaling ship seemed to be laboring under a cloud of its own making.

While David watched, the two men standing at the rail of the whaler took up the end of a rope that was tied around the waist of a third man. This man stepped over the side and stood on the whale's head, while a large iron hook was lowered to him on a chain.

Fascinated, David hopped up on the rail to get a better view. He clung to the rigging with one hand while with the other he shaded his eyes against the glare of the morning sun.

The man standing on the whale's head bent over and seemed to be doing something around the whale's jaw. A moment later he motioned for the iron hook to be lowered down to his feet. David guessed that he was inserting the hook through the whale's jaw before cutting the head free of the body. Sure enough, David could see the man reach up and receive a long, thick-bladed instrument, like a saw. The man began wielding this tool right behind the whale's head.

David strained to see even better, certain that there would be a dramatic moment when the head would be severed and would swing free of the carcass. In that instant, the man using the saw would be totally dependent on his shipmates holding the rope to stop him from plunging into the sea with the sharks.

A moment more passed. The man gestured for the chain to take up some slack. A few more deft strokes. Forward of David on the *Wanderer* came the cry, "The wind is rising. Now she fills!"

David tried to look three places at once: up at the sails no longer hanging limp overhead, over his shoulder at a cloud mass rushing down on them, and back at the sailor who was even then leaping for the railing to re-board the whaling ship. The *Wanderer* gave a lurch forward, then heeled sharply to starboard. David jerked once, then a second bounce sprung his grip loose. His new shoes, with their slick leather soles, accelerated his slide. Over the side he went.

Down he plunged into the dark blue water. Down he sank as the sea closed over his head. He kicked off his new shoes and struggled out of his new dress coat. It had so quickly filled with water that it threatened to carry him to the bottom.

Up he struggled and up, feeling as if his lungs would burst. At the last moment, when his tortured lungs could take no more, his head finally broke through the surface. He coughed, then breathed frantically, sucking in a huge breath before a swell broke over his head.

David raised his arm to wave to the *Wanderer*; he opened his mouth to shout and got a throat full of salt water. Kicking as hard as he could, he thrust his body up above the surface. Incredibly, the *Wanderer* was already two hundred yards away and increasing its speed. Had no one seen him fall?

"Wait!" he yelled. "I'm here!" He saw no move to slacken sail; heard no shouted order to come about.

For an instant, David panicked. He saw himself

alone, abandoned on the face of the deep. Then he remembered the whaler. He spun himself around, catching another wave in the face as he did so.

The whaler had been lying with its sails furled, willing to remain becalmed while it completed its industry of turning the whale into oil. Now that its task was nearly complete, it would return to the hunt—but leisurely, not racing ahead like the *Wanderer*.

David addressed himself to the whale ship, waving and shouting again. After an eternity, it seemed to David, a figure at the rail pointed in his direction, then called to another and another. Soon the rail was lined with men pointing and shouting.

David struggled to keep waving. His legs were tiring and he wanted to rest from the constant kicks upward, but was afraid he would disappear in the swells and be lost from view. He quickly stripped off his new linen shirt and flung it back and forth over his head. From around the opposite side of the ship came a whaleboat. As if already returned to hunting whales, it came on with the harpooner standing in the prow. Six men were pulling at the oars while an officer at the tiller shouted first to pull to larboard and next to give way as he followed the hand-signals of the brown-skinned harpooner.

The whaleboat had closed half the distance between them when David saw the harpooner stoop down and take up the eight-foot-long tool of his trade. The sunlight glinted off the razor-sharp edge.

What's he doing? screamed David's brain. *What's happening?* A moment later from the whaleboat he heard the exclamation of the oarsmen mixed with shrill cries from the watchers on the ship's deck. "Mano! Big shark! Big shark! Look at that fin!"

David's mind refused to accept this new information. Nearly drowned, and now a shark? It wasn't possible! Then he saw a scythe-like fin cutting through the water on a line directly toward him.

He began flailing wildly, slapping his shirt from side to side in a frenzy of terror. As if it were frozen in time, he saw a picture of the distance that still separated him from the boat, saw the shark's cold, lifeless eye stare into his, saw the harpooner's weapon drawn back, poised in his hand.

A frozen moment, but no longer—all was a rush of motion again. The shark's jaw closed on the shirt David slapped in its face as he jerked aside. The harpoon flashed forward, burying itself in the shark's body and making it curl on itself suddenly. David's plunge to the side had thrust him down in the water, and he choked, strangling and fighting, then lapsing into unconsciousness.

The whaleboat pulled past the thrashing shark. Strong hands lifted David into the boat and pounded him between the shoulders, but he couldn't see or feel them; he lay senseless in the bottom. As they pulled back to the whaler, all hands wondered if they had rescued a corpse.

David heard the distinct flapping of sails and then felt the warm sun begin to penetrate his wet clothes.

A broad, nut-brown face leaned into his view. A deep, resonant voice spoke in fluid Hawaiian tones, "Kawika. Kawika. You are safe now."

David tried to draw a deep breath, as if to prove that he was indeed still alive. Instantly, he was racked with coughing and retching as the remains of the sea water he had inhaled and swallowed tried to come up at once.

"Kawika!" said the voice again. Strong and gentle hands raised him to a seated position and thumped him on the back.

Trying again to focus his eyes and his thoughts, David was momentarily blinded by the sunlight. He still could not speak, but he raised one hand, palm outward, in a gesture of thanks—and to stop the pounding on his back.

David's mind raced as he turned to look at his benefactor. Who would know to call him by the Hawaiian version of his name? Who on this whaling ship could know him at all?

The man behind him moved around David and squatted down in front, blocking the sun's glare. A thatch of white hair crowned a large tan face with an enormous growth of side whiskers. The face split apart in a huge grin, revealing radiantly white teeth. The image of a coconut being suddenly cracked open flashed through David's thoughts. "Keo. Keo Kekoa?"

"Hey, Kawika," said the Hawaiian, "you pupule, or something? Crazy? What you go swim with old Mano for? You want end up in his opu?" Keo laughed exuberantly and patted his own ample belly.

"Keo," began David again. "I haven't seen you in five or six years, and now you save my life. That was you with the harpoon, wasn't it?"

"Sure, sure, Kawika. I been harpoon-man all this time here on Kilikila." He waved his hand to indicate the whaler. "The *Crystal*. Good whale ship."

A gravelly voice interrupted. "Stow it, Kekoa. Have your reunion later. Who is this wharf rat?"

David stood up to face the speaker. He found himself

looking down on a thin-faced man whose eyes appeared to have a permanent squint to match the perpetual sneer on his lips.

"I am not a wharf rat, Captain. I am a man of property *en route* to Boston, and if you'll put me back aboard—"

"Belay that guff. Have you got money?"

David shook his head. "No, of course not. Not with me. You can see I barely escaped with my life, but not my clothing. Back on the *Wanderer* is my letter of credit."

The sneer widened. "You talk fancy for island scum. Like enough you are a runaway cabin boy who jumped ship in Owyhee."

"Captain, I assure you, I have means."

"Avast that sea foam. Don't I have eyes to see you there all burnt brown like Kekoa here? You are no gentleman."

"But I . . . just recently I—" protested David lamely.

"You, Kekoa," addressed the captain to Keo, "you know this fella. Who is he now? Sail a straight course, or I'll pin your ears to the mast."

"Aye, Cap'n," said Keo, throwing a reluctant glance at David. "I speak true. Kawika here son of preacherman Kapono Bollin."

"Aha!" shouted the captain, his sneer fairly playing all over his face. "I mighta know'd. He was a stowaway, no doubt." The captain dismissed Keo curtly by gesturing aloft and ordering, "You heard the cry to make sail; now up the foretop with you."

"Aye, Cap'n," agreed the native. With a regretful look at David, he left to ascend the rigging.

The captain moved very close to David. "Preachers are useless spawn, and the spawn of a preacher is worse.

You may think fancy words make you better'n me, but look sharp! The *Crystal* is carryin' no cargo but oil—so less you want to fetch up shipped home in a cask, or thrown back to the sharks, you'll work for your keep, or my name isn't Captain Greaves."

————

The towering green peaks of Nu'uanu Pali were bathed in sunlight. Below, a blue mist hung, enfolding the valleys at the foot of the mountains. The dew sparkled on the short, crisp grass that carpeted pastures surrounding the village. Surf pounded on the shoreline a hundred yards from the white frame church of Kapono William Bollin.

How very close to paradise this place seemed! The laughter of brown-skinned children filled the air. In front of a small grass house, an old man labored to make fishing line from the fiber of beaten hemp. It was not hard to imagine the voice of the Lord as he looked upon this small corner of creation, *"Maikai, maikai; it is very good. . . ."*

Yet this morning, the beauty that surrounded Kapono Bollin only served to sharpen the depth of his grief as he read the contents of a letter from the captain of the schooner, *Wanderer.*

"And so it is my sad duty to inform you that your son was lost at sea, presumed drowned. There is some small hope, perhaps . . . a whaling vessel nearby . . . ."

The church bell pealed over the peaceful land, calling all the villagers to assemble. While Kapono Bollin retired to mourn in his house, assistant pastor Edward Hupeka stood before the congregation and translated the letter into Hawaiian.

The drone of insects accompanied the announcement in the packed room. Men and women, small children looked at one another in sorrow for the tearing of Kapono Bollin's heart. With a trembling hand, young Edward Hupeka placed the letter on the pulpit and looked out over the silent faces of his people. Tears filled his eyes. David had been like a brother to him once, yet David had not chosen the path of righteousness. He had rejected the truth his own father had taught. He had turned his back on the way of *Aloha*.

Edward turned his gaze onto the sad eyes of his sister, Mary. The small children of her class clung to her skirts. They looked worried. Mary was crying also. After all, she had loved David more than anyone.

Edward cleared his throat and began to speak. "Our brother is lost," he said, and his voice cracked. "What do we learn from such sorrow? *E imi oukou ia Iehova—* Seek the Lord while He may be found; call upon Him while He is near!" Heads bowed in thought and prayer as the voice of Edward rang out the warning. "Let the wicked forsake his way, and the unrighteous man his thoughts; let him return to the Lord, that He may have mercy on him, for He will abundantly pardon!"

"But perhaps Kawika still lives," said an old man near the pulpit.

"There was the whale ship nearby," cried another.

"We should pray that this is so. For Kapono Bollin, we should pray the boy still lives!"

"*No ka mea, o ko'u mau.*" For my thoughts are not your thoughts, says the Lord. Edward raised his arms and all the people began to pray together for their lost brother. For the lost son of dear Kapono Bollin.

CHAPTER 2

Three months later found David still aboard the *Crystal*. David's already tan body was burnt to a deeper brown, his blond hair bleached to a paler gold. His six-foot-three frame had filled out to a lean-muscled twenty from a boyish nineteen. His light green eyes reflected that he was stronger, more confident. Although he had acquired skills in the whaling trade, he still hated it all.

He had soon learned that life aboard a whale ship divided into only two categories: relentless boredom and punishing work. For days on end the *Crystal* cruised the whaling grounds with no quarry in sight. David's watches were usually spent hollystoning the decks. His knees and palms became thickly calloused until they felt like the soles of the shoes he had lost.

But even four hours at a time on hands and knees was preferable to being confined in the cramped forecastle. There, with little light and less air, those who knew scrimshaw engraved shark teeth and pan bones with fanciful scenes, while the others watched.

The only other recreation seemed to be griping. There was plenty to gripe about, too. The sailors warned David that it was well that they ate in the dark forecastle so as not to see the number of weevils in the bread.

David learned to swallow and keep down a drink

called *switchel*. Compounded of water dosed liberally with molasses and vinegar, it was less putrid than plain water that had stood in moldy barrels for forty days at a stretch.

David, like all the others, hoped and waited for the cry from the masthead, *There she breeches! There go flukes!* A sighting meant an injection of excitement into their boredom. It was soon ended, though, for the whale either escaped and the whaleboat crews came back to face Greaves' derision or else they towed the dead hulk back to the *Crystal* and their work began in earnest.

David was assigned to the "reception room," where huge blankets of blubber were cut into smaller pieces for the try pots. With malicious irony the captain had seen fit to require David to use the two-handled knife that cut the fat into thin squares called Bible leaves. Aside from the rough humor, it was a dangerous place to work. Razor-sharp blades were slicing in all directions in the cramped space, and sharp-spiked staves called blubber hooks gouged into the masses of fat without regard to legs or feet. David was the only man with all his fingers and toes working in the reception room.

Just as the flurry of activity was pushing the crew to the point of exhaustion, it ended. Back to the dull routine went the men, except that David's life was worse because all the surfaces he had just finished hollystoning were now covered again with a layer of grease. Grease that coated deck and rail, windlass and mast, whose removal was David's special duty. Very seldom did the *Crystal* resemble her name.

Greaves would not put David ashore until the *Crystal* returned to Honolulu for her semi-annual refitting. David dared not protest, because the only thing harder than the work of rendering a whale was the discipline.

Insubordination was punished by example: Greaves had not been joking when he threatened Keo with ear-pinning; David had seen a sailor pinned to the mast by a spike through his earlobe. The choice was to stand up for twenty-four hours in blazing sun or bone-numbing fog, or to pull out the spike and be lashed to unconsciousness.

Keo would pass David on the deck and whisper, "Ho' omanawanui. Be patient, Kawika." But he could seldom say more. The harpooners were considered to be a class above the common seamen, and for Keo and the young man to be openly friendly would mean trouble for both.

Many was the time David wished he had never left Hawaii, his self-pity often supplemented by anger. Then, perversely, he would blame his father for his predicament, unreasonably thinking that if they had returned to New England together, this would not have happened. At other times he missed his father and hoped that his father was praying for him.

Three months of this pattern went by, and the *Crystal* was coasting along the shores of California, far from the familiar beaches of Hawaii. She had put in for water at a wild stretch of the Baja Peninsula and was following the track of the gray whales north for a time.

Captain Greaves ordered the ship to lay in the lee of Santa Rosa Island until sundown. The *Crystal* would be heading windward to round Point Conception, and Greaves hoped the nighttime passage would make for calmer seas.

David was off-watch and below decks when the order came to make sail. As the canvas stretched and caught the wind, he could feel the *Crystal* shake herself like a dog getting up from sleep.

Once outside the shelter of the island, two things became clear to David: the wind had not died down as

expected, and the ocean swells were running from behind the ship, as if opposing the wind.

In order to progress to the northwest against the
wind, it was necessary for the ship to zigzag across the
intended course. The ship ran well enough on the leg in
toward land, but each time the *Crystal* put her helm over
to move west she came almost to a complete stop. David
experienced a sense of helplessness as he felt the ship
slide backward, pushed by the wind and overtaken by
the swells. Tension gripped the pit of his stomach as he
remembered a bit of sailor doggerel about a following
sea and a wallowing ship.

He overheard the mate Nelson being urged to query
Captain Greaves about breaking off the attempt and running back to shelter. Mentally he agreed. But when he
heard Greaves tell the mate to stop acting so childish
and return to his place, David felt his uneasiness return
even more.

Greaves ordered the steersman to put the helm over
once more and bring the ship up on the port or westward
tack, away from land. As he did so, David, who was sta-
tioned by the foremast, saw an unusual movement of the
timber. The mast not only bent and shivered, but seemed
to revolve part way around.

David's sense of danger increased to a certainty. He
tried to call this occurrence to the mate's attention, but
was curtly ordered back without a chance to explain. At
that moment the *Crystal* was passing to the west of Point
Conception and was no longer even partly sheltered by
the cape. The wind, which had been blowing at eighteen
knots, jumped up to forty. The tops of the onrushing
swells blew back into the faces of the *Crystal*'s crew.

"Captain!" shouted the mate over the roar of the wind
and the whine of the rigging. "Let her give way and run

downwind. We're making no headway at all!"

Greaves refused. He reasoned that if they held to their present course long enough, they would round the point. To give way now would drive them miles out to sea, just when the worst of the passage must be ending. What he did not know was that the south swells were being pushed out from a hurricane hundreds of miles away that was only beginning to gather its force. Outside the island channels, the swells were already increasing in height and force as if to compete with the wind.

David watched six-foot swells become twelve, then twenty. The ship became a plaything of the opposing forces that batted her back and forth. Shrouded by black skies in which the stars appeared to whirl like tiny candle flames about to be puffed out, the *Crystal* slid from crest to trough. Poised on the brink of a forty-foot hole in the ocean, blacker than the night itself, the ship, lifted by the onrushing swell, hung from the lip over a cavern into which thousands of tons of sea water were about to fall. Then the swell crashed past, while the *Crystal* slid backward into the trough. David looked up at a solid wall of water ready to fall on him.

Childhood prayers came to his mind. In a panic of gut-wrenching fear, he prayed for deliverance, prayed to be spared, offered bargains of reformation in return for life. He expected each moment to be the ship's last—and with it, his own end.

Now the mate was imploring the helmsman to keep her up into the wind. An instant's inattention could swing her broadside, to be rolled over and crushed.

"I can't hold her!" the steersman cried. Two burly sailors and Keo jumped to his aid. Together the four men struggled with the wooden spokes of the wheel to keep her nose up into the gale.

At that instant David saw the foremast revolve. "The mast is going!" he yelled, throwing himself back and out of the way. The starboard rigging parted with a sound like a dozen pistol shots and the foremast toppled over the portside of the ship.

Lines and yardarms snaking across the deck flipped men over the side like a giant flicking matchsticks. Two sailors were flung away without time to make a sound, while a third gave a horrible, drawn-out scream that followed his high arc into the sea. David shuddered as his mind told him that he might be next.

One of the try pots broke free of its brick oven and slammed a sailor against the gunwale. Then it spun off, as if seeking others to run down.

"Secure that cursed pot!" shouted Greaves, "and chop the foremast free!"

The foresails, and the jib which had been carried away with the mast, were hanging over the portside of the *Crystal*. The added drag threatened to spin the ship sideways into the canyon-like troughs.

Transforming panic and fear into frantic chopping, David snatched up an axe and began to cut at the rigging that still secured the foremast to the ship. His breathing was rushed and his arms rose and fell with the speed of a steam-driven piston. Other whaling men began to hack at the lines with their knives.

Presently the cry went up: "She's going!" The men jumped to get clear when the massive pole and acres of canvas fell free of the ship. The *Crystal* bounded to the starboard as the strain of the sails fell away.

Past the tip of Point Conception, the wind's direction shifted. While not letting up in force, it backed around to the northeast. Now the ship's motion toward the west came easier and she stood out from the land and rocks that had been waiting to tear out her keel.

As the *Crystal* limped along, the ship's crew were able to reef some sail, tying it down to take some of the strain off the rigging. The captain and the mate inspected the damage. The foremast was gone completely, and in the confusion the maintop had been carried away without anyone noticing. The rudder was damaged as well, making the *Crystal* very difficult to steer to starboard.

David experienced a strange welter of mixed feelings. He felt embarrassed for his time of panic and wondered if anyone had noticed him. He felt overwhelming relief at still being alive and a guilty shame because he was so glad that he was not one of those sailors lost overboard. He even associated his prayers in that time of fear with the foolishness of panic.

Below decks the scene revealed by cautiously lit lanterns was one of jumbled confusion. Several casks of oil had burst and the entire hold was soaked in a slippery coating. Fortunately, the barrels had not shifted or the *Crystal* would certainly have capsized.

As dawn broke over the coast range, the sailmaker was set to work stitching together spare canvas, and a jury-rigged boom was added to the stump of the mainmast. Greaves assured the crew that the *Crystal* could still be controlled in this way. What he did not report was how badly sprung the ship was, nor the fact that he was not sure how long she would hold together. A constant rotation of men kept the pumps going. David saw some of the more experienced sailors exchange knowing looks, but they made no comment. David did not even want to ask for explanation. He wanted no emotion except relief.

Where could they go for repairs? Clearly, they could not return the way they had come. The run northeast to the port of San Luis Obispo, which was the next closest shelter, was not possible either.

Monterrey seemed the logical choice. Captain Greaves was counting on the wind returning to the prevailing northwest direction in order to move the ship back toward the coast.

The following day was spent watching the beautiful but desolate central California coast slide by. The cleanup and repair work—but not the pumping—were suspended only briefly while the body of the man crushed by the try pot was consigned to the Pacific. The captain read no service and spoke no words. He merely stood in bareheaded silence for a moment before his curt nod caused the plank to be raised and the canvas-shrouded body to splash into the sea. David was standing next to Keo. Glancing over at the native, he saw that Keo's eyes were shut tightly and he was murmuring the words of the Lord's Prayer to himself in Hawaiian. David tried to force himself to follow suit, but his happiness at not being dead kept intruding. He'd just been lucky, that was all. The dead man had been unlucky.

By the middle of the next night, it was clear that the *Crystal* could not make port in Monterrey. She was now too far out from the coast and too damaged to move northeast against the wind. Their next—perhaps last—hope would be the tiny settlement of San Francisco, if the ship could be turned to make the narrow entrance into the bay.

Just after dawn on the second morning after the storm, the wind from the northeast died and the swells from astern shrank in size. The *Crystal* had at last outrun the effects of the Mexican hurricane.

CHAPTER 3

It was flat calm from six o'clock till nine. David paused in his work of splicing lines to gaze eastward at the yellow orb of the sun rising over the bank of gray fog that blocked his view of the coast.

Gently, almost imperceptibly at first, a breeze out of the northwest came up. The crippled whaling ship was being wafted in toward shore.

David's attention was caught by two cone-shaped masses that rose higher than the fog bank. He pointed them out to Keo, who was seated cross-legged on the deck nearby.

From the sling rigged to replace the vanished crow's nest, the lookout called, "Headland! Headland! Off the starboard beam!"

"Then we've made it?" asked David happily. "We're safe?"

He turned to find Keo looking serious rather than elated. "Not yet, Kawika, not yet. You feel how late *Kilikila* turns? I have been this Frisco place before. The tide moves very fast. If it falls we cannot enter, and if we catch the rise, then like the swiftest tuna we will swim. Only—" He paused and added soberly, "We cannot steer good."

Greaves had decided that there was no choice. He

directed the helmsman to hold a course between the headlands. Presently they entered the fog bank and were steering by compass alone. The fact that they were in the channel soon became apparent; the *Crystal* once again began to pick up speed. The tide was on the rise and they were committed.

A rocky cliff loomed up to port, and the *Crystal* was urged by the steersman's touch and the combined wills of all the crew back to the center of the channel. The fog swirled about the deck and through the makeshift rigging as the mist was also funneled through the mouth of the bay.

Every man aboard the *Crystal* seemed to be holding his breath. When would they make it through the narrows into safety? Would the fog break before they smashed into some unseen obstacle? David's eyes were strained to bulging as he tried to pierce the clammy curtain; his ear was keenly tuned to catch the sound of breakers on the unseen shore. He wanted this voyage to end, wanted desperately to be safe on land again.

No human sounds were heard for a time, and then a collective sigh went up. From the ruined prow of the *Crystal* to her battered stern, exhaled breaths of relief worked their way aft. As cleanly as parting a curtain and stepping from darkness into a lighted room, the *Crystal* sailed into the sunlit broad expanse of San Francisco Bay. The warmth on David's face was like a welcoming hug of safety and rest.

Even Greaves' shoulders relaxed a bit. "Let her have her head, helmsman. I'll have her run southeast around the point."

"Aye, sir," came the reply.

Passing between the rocky island shown on the 1847

chart and the peninsula containing the settlement still listed as Yerba Buena, the *Crystal* shaped her course toward the anchorage. The drifting fog still obscured the waterfront. Backslapping, congratulations, and a strange brew of profanity and prayers of thanksgiving erupted from the crew.

"Captain," came the call from the lookout, "ease her off a point. We'll have to pick our way through the ships ahead."

"Eh?" replied Greaves, his thoughts interrupted. "What ships? How many?" Even as this question echoed up the mast, Greaves' own eyes were supplying the answer, but his crew came to conclusions of their own.

"Forty ships! I count forty!"

"No, I make it seventy-five. See, there's another row over yonder."

"It's closer on a hundred!"

"What is it, Keo? Why are all these ships here?" asked David.

"I don't know, Kawika. War, maybe? Some angry storm coming, maybe? And something scare men away."

"What do you mean, Keo, scare the men away?"

"Look, Kawika," replied Keo, his muscled brown arm outstretched, "ships all malukia, too quiet. Sailors all gone!"

It was true. The ships appeared to be derelict. The harbor showed none of the expected activity—no loading or unloading of cargo, no ships preparing to weigh anchor, no small craft carrying men between the anchored ships and the shore. It was all eerie and ghostlike. Unpleasant memories of ship-born plagues and mass graves came to David's thoughts.

His gaze wandered to the shore, following the line of

his thoughts. The fog, already blown from much of the bay, still clung to the steep, knobby hills that made up the settlement of San Francisco. As he watched, the haze began to clear from the waterfront. At last the mystery of the deserted ships became clear—at least as far as the whereabouts of their crews. The waterfront was a bustling mass of activity, as busy with milling throngs of people as the ships were deserted. Past a line of larger, two-story shops, stores, and hotels, row upon row of haphazard-looking cabins climbed the hill behind the harbor.

As the *Crystal* slowed to a position at the end of a line of unmanned ships, David saw smoke rising from a hundred chimneys and stovepipes. On the muddy thoroughfare along the wharf, he caught glimpses of men passing with tools on their shoulders. He saw two men pulling the lead rope of a reluctant donkey while a third man pushed the animal's rump. A group of men passed, covered in blanket-like garments that reached to their knees. These same men were wearing wide-brimmed, low-crowned hats. David looked an inquiry at Keo, who merely shrugged and remarked, "Ha'i mai 'oe, Kawika, you tell me."

The anchor was let go and Captain Greaves, first mate Nelson, and one whaleboat crew prepared to go ashore. The others were ordered to remain aboard. There was some grumbling amongst the crew at this pronouncement, but no move toward open rebellion.

David was hopeful. "Perhaps one of these ships is the *Wanderer* with my letter of credit," he remarked to Keo. "Or perhaps at least someone has news of her. At the very least, I can work my passage back to Hawaii. Maybe my things were returned there."

David began scanning the rows of moored ships for the *Wanderer*. Behind him, back toward the mouth of the bay, he heard a signal gun boom. Another ship was entering the harbor.

Presently, out of the fog bank she came, looking clean, efficient and healthy, especially compared to the bedraggled *Crystal*. It was the side-wheeler *Fremont*, as the gold-lettered bow proclaimed. Her paddlewheels churned the waters of the bay as she steamed into view. Pennants were streaming from every masthead and an oversize American flag flew over the stern, its thirty stars gleaming proudly.

Even more remarkable to the sailors left on board the *Crystal* were the men lining the rail. The *Fremont's* upper deck was crammed shoulder to shoulder with men waving their hats and cheering. Keo and David exchanged questioning looks and waited as the *Fremont* blew a long whistle blast and drew up alongside. The crowd on the *Fremont's* deck could be seen picking up bundles and suitcases piled on the deck beside them.

"Some kind of hurry these haoles in, eh, Kawika?" commented Keo.

David nodded, "And look there, Keo. See how many of them have their bundles tied to picks and shovels."

David waved to a tall, frock-coated man carrying over one shoulder a pick from which hung a carpetbag. The man was wearing a stovepipe hat. Raising his voice to carry above the murmurs and rustles of the *Fremont's* passengers preparing to disembark, David yelled, "Ahoy! What's all the commotion about?"

"Don't you know?" shouted the tall man in reply. "Gold! Gold has been found upriver from here. We're all going to be rich as Croesus!"

"What?" yelled David. "Where's this gold?"

But the man could not be bothered to converse further. He was busy pushing past others who were still gathering their things. Soon his stovepipe hat could be seen in a lighter, dangerously overloaded boat, bobbing its way toward shore.

"Gold, Keo!" David exclaimed. "The stories I heard in Honolulu last winter were really true. There *is* gold in California. I can make my fortune here! What do I need Boston or a letter of credit for? I'll make my own riches."

"Kali iki, Kawika. Wait a little. Let us find out more." The news spread like wildfire through the men on board the *Crystal*. The word was on every tongue; visions of wealth swirled through each brain. *Gold!*

Some of the sailors on the *Crystal* were as impatient as David. While he and Keo were still watching the *Fremont* and discussing the exciting news, a group of whaling men piled into a boat and dropped away from the ship.

"Come back!" shouted the man Greaves had left in charge. "Be hanged," returned a sailor named Branch. "We'll no more sail with the reek of blubber, nor 'Squinty' Greaves. When next we sail, it'll be as kings and princes on our own yachts!"

David saw the whaleboat pulling toward shore meet up with Captain Greaves returning from the dock. Too far away to hear, David could only guess at the furious argument taking place as Greaves stood in one boat gesturing angrily. David watched as Branch rose in the other boat to reply. A moment later Greaves reached quickly inside his coat pocket, then withdrew his hand and extended his arm to point at Branch.

A puff of grayish-white smoke obscured Greaves' hand, and an instant later the report of a pistol cracked in the ears of the watchers. David could see Branch grasp his midsection with both hands before toppling suddenly backward into the water.

Three other men in Branch's boat leaped into the water, but no one had the idea of rescuing him. Instead, Keo and David saw them all strike out for shore, swimming as rapidly as they could.

Greaves gestured with his other hand. It must have contained another pistol, for soon both whaleboats and the remaining men could be seen pulling back toward the *Crystal*. As the boats tied up alongside, David could see that both Greaves and the mate were armed. The crewmen clambered aboard, closely watched by the two men with guns. David looked into each sailor's face as they climbed over the rail. He read there mixtures of fear, sullen anger, and greed, and he knew his own face reflected these qualities, too.

Greaves ordered the men onto the foredeck. When they were assembled and standing under the watchful guns of the officers, he began to address them.

"All right. You've heard the tales. While we were at sea, some madness about gold has set in. This port is lined rail to rail with lubbers thinking to make their piles." Greaves went on to explain how the gold seekers were all fools and how the real wealth lay in profiting from their madness.

"This whale oil that sells for 21 or 22 cents a gallon back in the States is fetching five times that much here! I intend to profit by this foolishness, and so shall you, but only if we get the *Crystal* refitted and get back to hunting whales!"

Greaves gestured angrily with his pistol at the hulks of abandoned ships. "These ships are mostly merchant vessels, derelict because their crews deserted. Well, by all that's holy, it won't happen to the *Crystal*! The master of the *Hartford* and others clapped their crews in irons to keep them from runnin' off. I won't do that, but you all are confined below decks till this madness settles and you see the wisdom of my thinking!"

An angry rumbling went through the crew at this, and some jostling forward. The mate looked frightened and backed up a pace, but Greaves merely waved his pistol and warned, "You saw how I served Branch. So shall all mutineers be served. All right now, speak up. Who wants some on their plate?"

No one spoke. "I thought not. All right, Mr. Nelson's watch is confined to the fo'c'sle. Get below there, now. The rest of you men, down in the hold with you."

David descended into the dark, greasy, evil-smelling hold, followed by Keo and the others. When the last one entered, Greaves clapped the hatches shut and ran the bolt home.

A man named Hughes called out then, "Hey, there's two feet of water in here, and oil on top of that!"

Greaves could be heard chuckling on the deck. "If you don't like the accommodations, then pray I strike a quick bargain for the cargo so's we can lighten ship before she settles right here at anchor."

David heard him call to the mate, "You have the watch, Mr. Nelson. I expect to be back shortly."

The men crammed into the hold could just barely make out the sounds of the oarlocks creaking as Greaves began to row back to shore. Suddenly everyone in the hold was talking at once.

"He can't do this!"

"That old pirate, who does he think . . ."

"How we gonna get outta here?"

"Let's rush him when—"

"Not me, brother! I don't want to be shot in the face. He'll do it, too. Look at poor old Branch!"

David took no part in these discussions, but his mind was racing. Certainly for the kind of money Greaves could obtain for the cargo, he'd be back with hired guards. If Greaves made good on his plan to force them to repair the *Crystal* and put to sea again, it could be another three months or longer before they had another chance at making port. And the gold! What about the gold? It must be real, and available in great quantity, to bring so many people so far from home!

David had seen his fortune, which had flown away on the departing sails of the *Wanderer*, come suddenly back within his grasp. If only he could get off this stinking ship! But how? What would make Greaves let them out at a time of enough confusion that he could slip over the side and swim to shore?

"A fire," he said aloud.

"Eh? What's that? Where?" remarked a startled sailor next to David.

"No, no. There's no fire. But listen, I have an idea."

Kco, who had heard those comments, called out in a booming voice that silenced the babble in the hold, "Be quiet, Kawika has an idea."

The other men gathered around and listened. David explained in quiet tones so that there was no chance of his plan reaching the ears of Nelson. The mate's footsteps could be heard echoing hollowly overhead as he patrolled the deck above.

When David was finished explaining, there was silence for a time, then nods of approval. "Is good, Kawika," Keo summed up. "We will follow your plan."

Greaves was gone a long time. The mate's worried pacing kept up all afternoon, describing small circles, then larger ones, then a circuit of the deck, and finally a pause at the landward rail to look for Greaves' return. Then the whole process began again.

On one of these circuits, David called out, "Mr. Nelson, how about letting us out of here?"

"I can't do that. Greaves would hand me my own head, right enough."

"But Mr. Nelson, we could take to the other boats and be lost in the city before he ever came back. Besides, what about the gold—gold enough to make all of us rich?"

In the gloomy shadows of the hold, the men could see reflected on all their faces the same eager, calculating looks they were sure appeared on the mate's face. For a long time he said nothing, and then responded, "No, it won't wash, men. You might escape, but he'd hunt me down for certain. Better we just wait and see what happens." David was disappointed and a little worried now that his plan would have to be used.

Enough curses to light the hold a sulphurous blue followed the mate as he resumed his stalking around the deck. Many a sailor promised himself to even the score with Nelson at the first opportunity, but David was fretting about Greaves.

It was evening before the splash of oars indicated Greaves' return. This timing was all the better for David's plan, and he went over it again with the sailors in hurried conference.

"All quiet, Mr. Nelson?" they heard Greaves inquire.

"Aye, sir," was the response.

"Now, you swabs hear me," shouted Greaves. "I've three armed men with me to see we have no more trouble. When I open the hatch, come up easy and I'll see you get fed. I've sold the whole cargo, and we'll all celebrate."

The bolt was thrown back and the hatch crashed open. Greaves stood and backed slowly away, gesturing with the pistol he held for the first man on the ladder to come up.

Keo and the other sailors first on deck saw that Greaves had spoken truthfully. Three grim-looking men circled around the hatch, each armed with a rifle and each carrying pistols and knives thrust into their waistbands.

"That's it, everybody come up easy like," instructed Greaves. "I'll unlatch the fo'c'sle now, and we'll all be one happy family again."

By this time, some fifteen men had exited the hold and were milling about, encircled by the guards. At that moment, still in the hold, David carefully ignited a greasy rag in a pan of oil and called out, "Fire! Fire in the hold!"

Others took up the cry, "Fire! The ship's on fire!"

The trick seemed to work. Greaves whirled about and ordered, "You men! Back down there double-quick and get the pumps going. Lively now!" Fire in the hold of an oil ship was a disaster all whaling men dreaded. David had counted on Greaves making an instant call for action without thinking that it could be a ploy.

The men really did turn back toward the hatch, which by now was venting dark, acrid smoke. The curious guards stepped in closer, not noticing that two whalers had moved particularly close to each of them.

Keo shouted, "Wela ka heo! Strike them now!"

Instantly, three wrestling contests began as two sailors grappled with each guard's rifle. Peering out of the hatch from the ladder, David saw a sailor shot at point-blank range as he grasped a rifle muzzle in an attempt to help. As the sailor fell back, the guard regained control of the rifle, and reversing it, swung it by the barrel in an arc that felled another whaler.

David gasped as one of the other guards lost the struggle for his rifle, and went down with a sailor's dirk protruding from his back. Greaves shot one sailor in the face, then began using his pistol as a club on anyone within reach, shouting for the mate to help him.

As David struggled upward on the stairs, Keo charged toward the mate, thinking to take him out before he could go to Greaves' aid. Nelson saw the Hawaiian rushing toward him, a belaying pin in his upraised fist like an ancient war club. The mate shrieked, discharged his pistol ineffectively into the air, and turned to throw himself over the side before the Hawaiian's blow could descend.

David sensed that the struggle could still be lost as the third guard released his hold on his rifle after shooting a sailor through the arm. He pulled a pistol from his belt, and brandishing it in front of him, waved the sailors back. He began to move, crablike, toward the rail, when his feet came within an arm's length of the hatch.

A sailor lunged out of the hold, grasping the guard around both ankles. Startled, the man discharged his pistol down into the deck, then toppled over backward, carrying both himself and the sailor down the steps into the hold. They tumbled over several others, including David. The pistol fire struck the oily casks, and they began to burn furiously.

A renewed, and this time, frenzied cry of "Fire! Fire!" went up, and there was a rush for the companionway. In the struggle for the stairs, the guard was trampled underfoot, drowned in the pool of muck in the hold.

David fought his way up the steps to find the remaining guard and Greaves fighting back to back on the deck. At the sight of flames shooting out of the hold and roaring up into the rigging, the guard and several of the whalers abandoned the struggle and threw themselves over the side without a backward glance.

Suddenly David stood face-to-face with Greaves. The captain was completely out of his mind; the crazed look in his eyes went everywhere, but focused on nothing. He snatched up a still-loaded pistol that had fallen to the deck and aimed vaguely at David. In the instant before firing, the captain found himself encircled from behind by Keo, and the belaying pin crashed down on his forearm. His shot caught David across the cheek—just grazing him, but raising a great, bloody welt from below his right eye to his ear. David's heart beat wildly; Greaves' face had taken on the coldly murderous expression of the shark.

Greaves just had time to fix David with a look of unutterable hatred before Keo picked him up. Two steps to the rail, and the native unceremoniously dropped Greaves into San Francisco Bay.

By now the fire was past extinguishing. The center section of the ship was engulfed in flames, and the stump of the mainmast was burning. Men all around were jumping into the water. David was preparing to leap also, when Keo laid a restraining hand on his shoulder.

"Wait, Kawika. You hear something?"

Above the roar of the flames devouring the *Crystal*, they heard cries for help. Agonized screams of terror were coming from the forecastle.

"Sailors still locked in fo'c'sle!" Keo cried. "Come on, Kawika, we must save them."

David looked at the flares of orange light erupting from the ship's deck and felt the heat on his wounded face intensify. He glanced at Keo's eyes and, for an instant, thought he read sorrow there. Then David swung his legs over the rail, and dropped into the bay.

CHAPTER 4

David gasped when he hit the water. Even in midsummer, the bay's temperature was icy. He struck out strongly for the shore, his direction plainly marked by the increasingly brilliant light thrown out by the blazing *Crystal*. A momentary shame at the thought of his cowardice made his face flush even in the frigid water, but he shrugged off the thought by the remembrance that he could still drown if he did not reach the shore soon.

David swam through a line of deserted ships. He thought of seeking shelter on one of them, but there was no one aboard to help him, and his increasingly numb fingers would not sustain his weight for a climb up the steep sides. He caught an anchor line and rested for a moment, panting from the exertion and shivering uncontrollably.

Up ahead he could see lights in the windows of a building. It was much nearer than he had supposed the shore to be, just behind a ship that was docked across a narrow channel from him.

David struck out again with renewed strength, anxious to get to land. When he was ten yards from the dock he began calling for help, but the noise and music from the lighted windows of the nearby building drowned out his cries. He clung to a piling, oblivious to the damage being done to his hands by the rough barnacles and mussels. David looked briefly for a ladder, but found none.

He resolved to pull himself piling by piling around to the shore side of the dock. Soon he reached the hull of a ship that he thought rested between him and the building on the shore. The ship *was* the building! Above its decks rose a makeshift three-story structure. Surrounded by docks and permanently fixed in the San Francisco Bay, it had been turned into a floating gambling hall, still fifty yards from shore.

A bumboat ferrying passengers out from shore to the gambling hall was arriving. Its occupants heard David's calls and assisted him from the water.

"Bit cold for swimmin', ain't it, young feller?" remarked the boat's skipper. He brought David a blanket to wrap up in.

Through chattering teeth, David explained about the fire onboard the *Crystal*. Several of the new arrivals strolled around the plank walkway to observe, but no one seemed very excited or made any move to get help. Now safe himself, David tried to urge these men to assist the *Crystal*.

"We don't get too excited about ship fires here, boy," explained the bumboat's operator. "Most of these ships is abandoned an' rottin' away. Shoot, Frisco has at least one fire a day—an' that's on a slow day. Why, we can't be runnin' off to put out no burnin' boats where they can't hurt nothin' by burnin' anyways."

"But there may be men trapped on that ship!" exclaimed David, feeling remorse now and worried about Keo.

"I'm sorry son, but you just take a peek at that blaze. She's burnt 'most to the waterline already. We're fixin' to put out again to pick up swimmers like yourself. Don't worry none. You go on in the *Bernice* here and warm yourself up."

David took the skipper's advice and, still wrapped in the blanket, made his way up a gangplank and into the converted ship-saloon.

Inside lay a scene of mammoth confusion, both of sight and sound, not to mention the smell of liquor and the all-pervading smoke that filled the room like a low-lying cloud.

The entire lower floor was one large room, filled almost entirely with tables crowded by gamblers, except along the wall opposite the entrance, which was occupied by a bar. David was stunned to see a portico of marble pillars behind the bar—until he realized that the scene was painted on the wall.

Near the center in front of the bar stood a group of bearded men with long, shaggy hair. They wore high-topped boots that reached to their knees and talked animatedly, between puffs on cheroots, about the good prospects of a place called Little Rich Bar.

On the left, as David faced the counter, stood three men dressed like those he had seen from the deck of the *Crystal*. They sported pointed beards and carefully groomed mustaches, and were covered front and back by a blanket-like garment through which their heads protruded. They were speaking a language David took to be Spanish, although he couldn't understand a word.

At the opposite end of the bar stood a pair of Chinese men. Their pigtails hung down below broad, flat straw hats with small pointed crowns. Apparently they could be understood by the bartender; as David watched, one of the Chinese reached inside his green silk jacket and retrieved a small bag. The barkeeper helped himself to several pinches of something from the bag, which he deposited carefully in a similar pouch behind the bar, then took down a bottle from the shelf behind him and set it and two glasses in front of the Chinese.

Dripping wet, barefoot, and penniless, David was unsure how to proceed or what to do with himself. He decided to address the bartender as being the only one present in any kind of official capacity. To approach the bar, David picked his way through intent circles of gamblers, stepping over a drunk lying full-length on the floor snoring, and carefully skirting a pile of shattered glass.

"Save your breath, friend," anticipated the bartender. "Drinks for gold either pinch or coin. No greenbacks and no credit."

Before David could even respond, the loudest of the bearded prospectors whirled around and confronted the white-aproned saloon man. "Say, barkeep, that weren't neighborly. Not neighborly a'tall. You must be tryin' to ruin this town's repute for friendliness."

"Strawfoot, are you willing to vouch for this fellow?" quizzed the bartender. "He's wrapped in a blanket like some Indian, he's been in a knife-fight or somethin', and he's almost without pockets to put money in—*if* he had any money, which I strongly doubt."

The man addressed as Strawfoot reached into a deep outside pocket of his faded blue knee-length coat and drew out a leather pouch like those David had already seen. "Here, young fella," he said, pitching the pouch to David. "I imagine that'll earn you a little respect." With no more comment or attention than this, he turned back to his interrupted conversation and instantly resumed arguing the respective merits of something called long-tom versus something else called rocker. He might as well have been speaking Spanish—or even Chinese—for all David understood of the debate.

David was astounded, and it must have shown on his face, because he looked up to see the bartender grinning broadly at him. He glanced away quickly and furtively loosened the drawstring on the pouch, half-expecting Strawfoot to snatch it back.

Reaching in with thumb and forefinger, David drew out a fine-grained, flaky powder that glinted dully in the light of the oil lamps. Leaning over the bar, the saloon-man said, "That's enough to buy you a drink. Five like that, and you can keep the bottle."

Nodding slowly in bewilderment, David deposited the pinch of gold dust in the bartender's outstretched hand and accepted a glass of whiskey in return. David tossed down the fiery liquor, choking back an urge to gag. He swallowed hard twice, then unclenched his eyes and teeth.

David held the pouch up and felt its substantial weight. He looked questioningly at the bartender, who gestured for David to hand it over. The bartender weighed the sack in his hand and considered briefly, then remarked, "Eight ounces, I judge. Worth, oh, a hundred and twenty dollars or so."

With that he passed the bag back to David and turned to answer a call for "Mo' whiskey" from the Chinamen down the counter.

David was flabbergasted. He started twice to tap Strawfoot on the shoulder and twice drew back uncertainly. Finally he collected himself and said in as firm a voice as he could manage, "Mr. Strawfoot—"

The bearded miner turned and regarded David with

GRABILL MISSIONARY
CHURCH LIBRARY

a smile. "Just Strawfoot. No Mister to it."

"All right, Strawfoot. My name is David Bollin, and I . . . I don't know quite what to say. I mean, we don't know each other, and yet the bartender tells me what you've handed me is worth over a hundred dollars in gold. Sir, you should know that I can't say when I'll be able to repay you, or how."

"Forget it. It weren't a loan, anyway." The hairy miner looked David over. "Appears that you are a mite down in your luck. Well, I been down, an' folks has helped me before. I just like to return the favor. Besides," Strawfoot continued, "it ain't so much. I come to this town with five thousand dollars to spend, an' I ain't leavin' till she's gone. You just helped me out a scooch."

Strawfoot seemed willing to continue the conversation, but he must have noticed something about David's wounded face or a waver in David's stance that concerned him, because he stopped abruptly. Leaning closer he asked, "You feelin' all right, son?"

"Just a little weak, is all," David replied.

"Shore, shore. Ice cold bath, somebody playin' merry ned with your cheek, and then a glass of this rat poison they serve for liquor. Fine doctor I am. Like to kilt you, no doubt."

Strawfoot called the bartender over. He gave instructions that David was going to use his room, and that the barkeep would please see that David got upstairs safely.

Over his protests, David was escorted upstairs and put to bed. As he fell asleep, his mind was a whirl of blazing ships, icy water, Keo, Strawfoot, and gold. Gold! Gold by the bagful, in shiny glittering heaps!

When he woke up the next morning, David couldn't immediately place where he was. At first he wasn't sure that the events of the day before had been real and not some unbelievably complicated dream. Then he put his hand up to his face and winced as his fingers touched the puckered wound that stretched five inches across his cheek. The fingers of his other hand closed around a small leather pouch, its drawstring still looped around his wrist just as he had placed it the night before.

A long rasping snore from close by interrupted his thoughts and made him clutch the pouch of gold even tighter. Cautiously David raised up from the pillow to look over the side of the bed. There, still fully clothed and stretching his six-foot length on the floor, was his benefactor, Strawfoot. Every time the miner breathed, his bushy black beard rustled like palm fronds in a high wind.

David's stomach growled, reminding him that through yesterday's confinement in the hold of the *Crystal* and all that followed, he had had nothing to eat. There should be more important things to think about, but David's hunger asserted itself, and his stomach growled again, louder this time.

This new noise had a curious effect on Strawfoot. His snoring stopped, replaced by a slurred mumbling. "Dang grizz. After that haunch a' venison. Bang some pans, somebody."

Apparently Strawfoot decided that no one was going to follow his instructions, so he sat up abruptly as if intending to see to it himself. He blinked widely three or four times, then added an enormous yawn and a stretch to his waking-up motions. He turned to regard David equably, without any of the confusion that had plagued David's waking.

"Good mornin'. You awake, too? You're looking some

better—least you're gettin' some color back. Last night you was so pale, that cut on your cheek looked like somebody writ with red ink on white paper."

David explained that he was indeed feeling much better, and that he was sorry to be occupying Strawfoot's bed while the miner slept on the floor.

"Think nothin' of it," was the prospector's reply. "Just bein' indoors with a roof over my head is a whole lot better'n other places I've slept.

"Say," Strawfoot continued, "are you hungry?" David's stomach growled again in reply. Addressing himself to the noise just as if David had spoken, Strawfoot agreed, "Well all right then, let's get goin'."

David vaguely remembered the bartender helping him out of his soggy shirt and dungarees the night before. Now he found them hanging over the foot of the bed, dried, if not any improved in quality. In a single moment David, with all his earthly possessions, was ready to travel.

"Where can we get breakfast?" inquired David.

"We could feed here on the *Bernice*," commented Strawfoot, "but I've got a hankerin' for oysters an' eggs, an' there ain't no better place for that than the Atlantic Hotel. Let's get goin' an' see if we can roust out that scoundrel of a ferryboat skipper."

Strawfoot's comments reminded David that he was still in the bay on a ship of sorts. This thought made his worry for Keo surface again strongly.

"Strawfoot, I need to go look for a friend. He . . . he was in the same ship fire as me last night and I, that is . . . We got separated . . ." His voice trailed off.

Strawfoot tried to cheer him up. "Why, we heard all about it. A bunch of your sailor friends was pulled out of the water here last night, an' a bunch more got picked up an' taken ashore. You needn't worry, I'm sure your friend is all right."

"Really?" asked David hopefully.

"Shore," came the reply. "An' what a grand fire it was, too! Some a' that burnin' oil spread over to a couple other ships. We was makin' bets on which one would burn the quickest!"

"I can't believe it!" exclaimed David, alarmed to find just how far his original plot had gotten out of hand.

"Nothin' to be upset about. The *Fremont* got up steam and moved out of the way. Whatever burned was just rotten hulks anyway. Come on, let's go eat, then we'll have a go at huntin' up your friend."

Outside on the dock David and Strawfoot found an arriving bumboat loaded with men eager to drink and gamble even though it was only mid-morning. "I ain't headed for shore just now," the boat's operator explained. "All these fares is comin' from the steamer anchored over yonder that's just in from Sacramento."

The pilot suggested that they go down to the end of the dock. "There's a boat tied up there with a feller sleepin' on it. Likely you can hire him to take you to shore."

As the small boat came into view David commented, "That looks like one of the whaleboats from the *Crystal*. And that man lying across the seats looks like—it is! Keo! Keo, wake up!" David ran the rest of the length of the dock shouting and waving.

Keo bounded up out of the whaleboat and grasped David in a hug that would have crushed several ribs had he not stopped when he did. "Kawika! you safe. I paddle all over looking for you."

Another pang of shame went through David. While

he had been inside sleeping, his friend had been out searching for him!

"But the fo'c'sle, the men there—" stammered David.

"Oh, everybody get off all right," reported Keo. "I even have time to lower last boat and help sailors out of bay. I keep looking for you but not finding."

David hung his head. "I know, Keo. I was already here, safe."

"Is good!" shouted the native. "Now everything is maika'i. All just fine now!" Keo looked at Strawfoot and the miner returned the gaze.

"This new friend, Kawika?" asked the Hawaiian, indicating the miner.

"What? Oh, yes. Strawfoot, this is the friend I was telling you about, Keo Kekoa. Keo, this is Strawfoot. He sort of took me in last night."

"Is good you help Kawika," said Keo sincerely. "Keo be friend to you, too. Say, Kawika, Pololi au! I am very hungry. Is food near here?"

"That's just where we was headin'," offered Strawfoot. "In fact, if you can get this boat goin' again, we'll go tie into some breakfast right now." Strawfoot paused as a thought struck him. "Unless, a'course, you're one of them cannibal fellas. I don't know where they cater to that whim!"

Keo laughed and thumped the miner so hard on the shoulder he almost knocked him off the dock. "No worry. I not hungry for tough haole covered in wire brush!"

The Atlantic Hotel turned out to be another ship converted into building, this one up on the shoreline and hemmed in on either side by more conventional structures. To reach it, the three companions had to slog down a planked road that was more mud than planks. Anyone who stepped off the planks sank to the knees, so most passersby resorted to jumping from board to board in a curious kind of hopscotch.

"I hear tell there's a whole freight wagon down under this somewheres, an' a Irish teamster still tryin' to get his mules to goin'," commented Strawfoot.

"I think I believe it," puffed David, pausing between leaps. "What do they call this triumph of engineering?"

"This highway is known as Market Street," replied the miner, leaping over to the ladder that rose from the mud to the deck of the Atlantic Hotel.

The foredeck of the Atlantic still had its mast in place. A sign tacked up near the gangplank read, "Here Laundry Done. You Wait," as an industrious group of Chinese scurried around scrubbing clothes and running them up the rigging to dry. Somewhat less wordy, but more enticing to David was a large sign reading simply "EATS," with an arrow pointing aft.

Over a meal in which the men consumed three entire skillets of scrambled eggs and oysters, they exchanged stories about past lives and future plans.

David said little about leaving Hawaii. Instead, he focused his attention on the gold fields, bombarding Strawfoot with a string of questions.

Strawfoot related that he had already been in California when the gold strike was first reported. He had been in the army, he said, and had elected to stay in this new country when he mustered out. He owed his unusual name to his army experiences as well. Soldiers who didn't know left from right were taught to march with a wisp of hay tied to one foot and a twist of straw on the other. The drill sergeant kept time by shouting, "Hayfoot, strawfoot, hayfoot, strawfoot." Most learned to march properly, but the bearded miner reported sheepishly that he never had quite gotten the hang of it and had received a permanent nickname as a result.

"I was headed for Coloma when I learned about a new strike a ways south of there. Seems some fellers named McCoon and Daylor took out, oh, seventeen, eighteen thousand dollars in one week. 'Well sir,' I said to myself, 'that's good enough for me.' "

"And did you strike it rich right away?" inquired David eagerly. "Is it really that easy?"

Strawfoot leaned back in his chair, clearly enjoying the rapt attention of his audience. "Hold on a minute, while's I wet my throat." He called the waiter and requested a "stone fence." When he explained to David that it was a mixture of whiskey and apple juice, David opted to try one also, but Keo declined.

When the drinks had arrived and been partly consumed, Strawfoot resumed his narrative. He explained that he had gone directly to an unoccupied section of a stream that was "no wider than this here table," which he had selected completely at random. He told how he had begun digging in the dry soil of the creek bank, shoveling out loose soil and stones to get down to bedrock. It had taken him four hours to get down four feet.

"I seen there was a crack in the rock face running alongside the creek. It were a space about as big across as my three fingers together." Strawfoot held up a gnarled and calloused hand to demonstrate.

After another swallow of his stone fence he continued, "That crack was packed with pea gravel and clay, so I taken my knife and went to scrapin' out that crack." He drew a broad-bladed knife almost ten inches in length from a sheath at his side and tossed it on the table.

"When I got to the bottom of that crack, what do you suppose I found?" Again Strawfoot stopped, and looked back and forth between his listeners with snapping dark eyes.

Slapping a meaty hand down on the table, Keo demanded, "H'ai mai! Tell us what!"

"All along the bottom of that space were a whole row of gold! Little kernels of gold, 'bout the size of apple seeds." Strawfoot fished an apple seed out of his drink, and laid it in his palm. The other two men leaned over to inspect it as carefully as if it were really a gold nugget.

"That first day's work weighed up to be close on fifty dollars, an' that was just the beginning."

David's heart was beating so fast that his voice sounded wavery when he asked, "And is there more left?" He tried to not breathe, so as to hear the reply clearly.

"Shoot, yeah. Most all prospectors plan to make their piles and skedaddle for home. I got no family and no home to go back to, so after I prospects a piece I come to town to celebrate. After all, what good is it if you can't spend it?"

David's heart wrenched at the words "family" and "home," but he quickly shoved those sensations aside. He wanted no sloppy sentiment to interfere with his becoming rich.

"How does one come to the country of gold?" asked Keo. "Is it far?"

"It's a pretty fur piece upriver," acknowledged the prospector. "Most fellas with money goes by boat as far as Sacramento. Them that can't afford passage gets across the bay here anyway they can, then they goes to walkin'!"

"'E!" exclaimed Keo. "We already have a boat. Since

Kilikila burn, I do not think Captain will be paying my six months' share. I think I keep whaleboat."

"Say, that's right. Strawfoot, would you like to travel with us? That's the least I can do for your kindness," offered David.

"Fair enough. Fact is, I was fixin' to ask you two to partner up with me," responded Strawfoot. "Unless," he added suspiciously, "you think I'm gonna help *row* all the way up to Sac."

"No, no! Keo can rig a sail, can't you Keo?"

"Pono! You bet!" agreed the Hawaiian.

Strawfoot advised David to buy supplies in San Francisco rather than wait to get them upriver. He explained that a $25 barrel of flour would cost $50 in Sacramento and climb to $100 at the diggings. They reviewed together the items needed and the quantity of each—flour, sugar, coffee. Picks, shovels, pans, stout knives, and at least one firearm for providing camp meat. Strawfoot headed back to collect his things and spend one more night "whooping it up" on the *Bernice*, while David and Keo set out to gather their supplies and see a little more of San Francisco.

CHAPTER 5

Several hours of shopping later, David and Keo had all their equipment and provisions purchased, wrapped securely in canvas, and stored aboard the whaleboat. Out of Strawfoot's gold dust, they had just enough left for dinner, one night's lodging, and breakfast before sailing.

"It doesn't matter, Keo," commented David confidently. "By the time this store runs out, we'll be as rich as King Kamehameha."

More out of a sense of curiosity than either the ability or the desire to participate, the two friends entered the Eagle Saloon and Gambling Parlor. Their attention was first captured by the barker who stood out front chanting, "Here's the place to win it all back! Step right up, gentlemen, find the lady and win two ounces. Yessir, you heard right. Wager one ounce and win two!"

From outside, the Eagle looked no more substantial than any of the other hurriedly built wooden structures forming what was euphemistically called the business district. It was sandwiched between a building with a sign proclaiming "Cheap Publications" and a structure announcing itself to be the headquarters of Epic Fire Company #1.

David was intrigued by the shoddy construction of

so populated a city. Honolulu was a much more substantial place, with several imposing stone structures and a sophisticated society—even if he, as a preacher's son, had never belonged to it. San Francisco felt like an extension of the wilderness, pretending to be a city. For all the saloons, shops, and other establishments, he had not seen one school. Honolulu had three.

He was snatched from this reverie when the barker addressed him directly. In his new flannel shirt and canvas pants, tucked into still-shiny new boots, he looked like a man of substance.

"Come in sir, come in. Finest establishment of its kind in the world. Come in and sample our Queen Charlottes—the best anywhere. The first is on the house. Yessir, right this way."

David looked at Keo, who shrugged agreement and the two made to enter. Seeing this, the barker dropped his loudspeaker voice and caught David by the arm. "Hold on a minute there, friend. Your partner here. He's not Indian, is he? Or Negro?"

David looked startled for an instant, then replied, "No, he's Hawaiian, and so—" He stopped midsentence and choked off the words, "am I."

The barker looked relieved. "Well, that's all right then," and added doubtfully, "I guess."

David and Keo went on into the saloon. David looked at Keo out of the corner of his eye to see if the islander showed any reaction. David thought perhaps Keo's jaw looked a little tighter than usual, but then decided he was imagining it. *Why didn't I finish saying that I was Hawaiian, too?* wondered David to himself.

In an attempt to change the subject of his thoughts, David said to Keo, "What is a Queen Charlotte, do you suppose?" When Keo did not reply, David shifted his attention to the gambling table just inside the entrance.

"Find the lady, gentlemen. That's the name of the game." The three-card monte dealer kept up a running patter while slapping three red-backed cards around in rapid motion. Over, under, under, over, the cards flew past each other, while an occasional flick of the wrist revealed the location of the queen of hearts before it rejoined the shuffle with the two jacks.

There were plenty of other games of chance operating in the Eagle. A large wheel of fortune was set in motion with a practiced hand, while miners placed bets on a hand-lettered board. Several faro tables were in use as well, but David didn't understand the game and soon drifted up to the bar.

"I'll have a, what do you call it? A Queen Charlotte." "Yessir," the bartender responded. He picked up a large tumbler and began pouring into it from two bottles at once. David saw that it was compounded of red wine and raspberry syrup. "On the house," the bartender confirmed, setting the drink in front of David.

David took a sip. It was amazingly sweet, and so heavy with syrup as to be gagging. David set the drink down and said for the bartender's benefit that it was very good, but he guessed what he was really thirsty for was a stone fence.

The bartender obligingly set up the requested concoction, then accepted a pinch of gold dust from David's dwindling supply. Aside to Keo, David remarked, "I can skip breakfast tomorrow and eat some of our crackers on the boat."

"Come on, Kawika, let's go now," advised Keo.

"You go on, if you want to," remarked David. "I'm

not through looking around here yet."

Keo murmured something about still needing to rig the sail for the whaleboat and turned to leave.

David felt a kind of relief when the native was gone. He didn't stop to think about it, but he wanted to get over his embarrassment. David downed the rest of his drink and called for another. Picking it up from the bar, he began to inspect the gambling tables again.

David's attention was particularly caught by one dealer who appeared flashier than the rest. This man was clean-shaven. He wore his receding dark hair long and combed back from his face; four of his ten fingers gleamed with rings, and he wore a shiny stickpin.

The dealer continued weaving the three cards in their rapid and intricate pattern, then stopped to place each one carefully in a box drawn for it on his green felt working surface. He took a moment to cover each card with his hand and straighten it so that its edges were exactly aligned with the box.

He then called for the bettor's decision as to the location of the queen. In contrast to the continuous flow of instructions, encouragement, compliments, and other patter that had come from the dealer, the opposing gambler was a silent man. He was studiously inspecting the backs of the cards as if he could read their identity through the pasteboard.

At last he reached a decision and placed a gold half-eagle in front of the center card. With a careless flick of the wrist and a small smile, the dealer turned over the chosen card to show that it was, in fact, a jack. Before collecting the money, the dealer took a moment to cover each card as before, carefully aligning the edges. He then turned over the card on the gambler's left, revealing the location of the queen.

The miner swore softly but acknowledged the dealer's right to pick up the coin. David saw him reach into his inside coat pocket and draw out another coin, this time a twenty dollar double-eagle. The man held on to the coin for a moment, eyeing it thoughtfully. At last making up his mind, he placed it on the edge of the table.

The dealer's patter began as before, and the cards resumed their mesmerizing flight. David had to force himself to avoid either listening to the dealer's words or looking at the flashing rings. Instead, he tried to concentrate on the cards alone. Each time the queen was turned up, David checked to see if his guess would have been correct, and he concentrated entirely on following that one card.

When the shuffling ritual was done and the cards again perfectly aligned, David was certain he knew the location of the queen. He and the man gambling apparently agreed, for the miner staked his double-eagle on the right-hand card without any hesitation.

For a bare moment, a flash of white from the dealer's palm caught David's attention. The dealer turned up the required card with practiced assurance, revealing that the miner had lost again. The miner shrugged, and prepared to stand and leave.

Almost without thinking, David interrupted. "Before you straighten the cards again, could I see the one in your hand?"

The dealer stiffened and made no move to bring his left hand up to the table. Instead, his right hand moved across his chest, reaching toward his coat. The miner who had just lost his money was paying close attention and moved faster than either the dealer or David.

The miner yanked a Bowie knife from his boot top and pinned the dealer's coat sleeve to the table. From the dealer's other hand a card floated free. The queen of hearts landed face up and smiling on the floor. There were still three cards on the table top. All three were jacks.

A brawny hand clasped around the dealer's throat and he stopped trying to free his imprisoned coat sleeve. As David watched, fascinated at the scene being played out in front of him, the prospector reached inside the dealer's coat. Thumb and forefinger lifted a single shot .44 caliber derringer from the coat pocket. The sight of the pistol made David's face twitch. He put up a hand and gingerly touched the crease made by the bullet wound—was it just the night before?

A crowd of gamblers had gathered around the table to watch, and as the proof of the cheating was revealed they began to murmur, "String him up."

"That's it, hang him."

"He was goin' for his gun, too. Lousy cheat!"

The owner of the Eagle came rushing over. "Gentlemen, please," he requested, "let's not have any bloodshed here. Right, sir?" He addressed himself to the miner who still held the dealer off the ground by the throat.

The prospector shook his head in disgust. "Turn out his pockets," he growled.

Several others jumped to obey this instruction. Like a chicken being plucked, the man was swiftly stripped of coat, vest, and pants.

When the dealer was left standing in his underwear and boots, a money belt he wore strapped around his middle was added to the pile of gold dust pouches and coins on the table. The humiliated dealer gasped out a feeble protest, "Most of these winnings were fair!"

"So, how about it, boys?" the miner addressed the crowd. "This cheat says he's bein' robbed. Do we believe him?"

A chorus of, "No. No way a'tall," and a renewed demand to hang the man rang out from the crowd.

"He's too scrawny now that he's plucked," concluded the prospector, echoing the same image that had occurred to David. "Just don't ever let me lay eyes on you again," said the miner, and he roughly threw the cheater to the floor.

The man started to stand up, but a well-placed kick stretched him on the floor again. Once there, he decided that crawling toward the exit would be safest. He did make it out the door, but not before a few more boots had connected with his posterior.

The miner turned to David. "I'm obliged to you, son. I imagine that I lose more than I win, but even so, I don't like bein' cheated."

David refused the miner's offer to split the money with him, but accepted the derringer. The prospector examined the money belt and seemed to find it to be fair compensation. He swept the odd change into a pile on the table and called out, "Drinks for everyone till we use it up." With whoops of delight the crowd expressed their agreement.

Fortunately for David, the Eagle was only a few blocks from his hotel. Several stone fences later, David had to have two new found friends help him back to his room. There he found Keo waiting for him, and he was soon asleep.

Even though he had been caught cheating this time, Owen Barton, the dealer, was a clever man—too clever, some folks said, and sharper in his business dealings than was good for his trading partners. The news of the strike in California had been truly a golden opportunity for him. The gold rush wasn't exactly the deciding factor in his leaving Saint Joe, Missouri. His neighbors had decided that for him when they concluded they'd been swindled enough. But the gold rush did decide the direction of his departure, a destination full of promise for a man who made his living cheating other people out of theirs.

Barton was a tall man, his stature accented by a high forehead and straight nose. He was vainly proud of his looks, despite his receding brown hair and his pockmarked face. He oozed persuasion as a maple tree oozes sugary sap. He could pretend to be a sharp-tongued Yankee or an aristocratic Southerner—whatever the circumstances called for.

Selling land he didn't own, hocking shares in fictitious businesses, or touting marvelous inventions that hadn't been invented yet were all part of his portfolio, but his day-to-day subsistence came from gambling. He was a cardsharp of the first water. Barton knew faro, fantan, monte, and poker, which he despised. Poker allowed a degree of skill to be made use of by Barton's opponents. He wanted only chance, greed, and his own subtle influences to affect the outcome.

He had gambled his way down the Mississippi and cheated his way across Panama. Once on the Pacific side, he had duped the skipper of a schooner into carrying him to San Francisco for free, courtesy of a rigged hand of three-card monte.

He had gone no farther toward the gold diggings than San Francisco, because he saw no reason to chase gold already coming to him. A few months raising capital with his gambling, and he would be all set for something more profitable and refined. San Francisco was ripe for a land scheme of some sort. After all, real estate values were already starting to soar.

But a moment of inattention on his part, together with too much attention by a sharp-eyed busybody, and Barton's plans had come unravelled. He had made a really stupid blunder with the monte game in the Eagle Saloon. Barton upbraided himself savagely for his slip. For a man who had been palming cards all his adult life, he could not believe how clumsy he had been.

Reaching for the derringer had been another stupid mistake. He should have distracted the miner somehow and rearranged the cards. If only, if only . . .

Yet Barton knew that he was lucky to be alive. The brand of justice served up in San Francisco was to hang men from lampposts—except that there were no lampposts yet. But he had seen men hanged from ships' masts and cargo cranes.

With the perverse logic of the chronically criminal and habitually lucky, Barton felt that he had been abused. To have all his gold hijacked was a terrible blow to his plans. To be stripped of his clothes and kicked into the street was an indignity past bearing.

Barton frowned and shook his head as he reviewed his circumstances. It was *almost* past bearing. The threat to his life was real if he remained in San Francisco: a new scheme would have to be developed—and quickly.

He ducked into one of the shabbier establishments. Shabbiness was relative in San Francisco, but the

Weathereye Tavern catered to seamen who had no gold to speak of and preferred their liquor potent and cheap. There were no Queen Charlottes in the Weathereye. Captains in need of replacement crews had been known to furnish rum in quantity for men who would wake up miles from land the next morning.

The bartender glanced up at the sight of the normally dapper gambler crossing the saloon in his underwear, but said nothing. Not only was the bartender naturally cautious, he had also been in Frisco long enough to know that much more unusual sights were possible.

Barton took the stairs to the second floor two at a time. He pushed into a room and shut the door quickly behind him. The slam of the door brought the tenant of the room to partial waking.

Lying on the rudely framed wooden bed, for which a salvaged sail served as both mattress and blanket, lay a man. He started up with his hand already grasping a Walker Colt. His saggy, jowled face was puffy with too much drink and too little sleep.

"What the—? What's the idea bustin' in here, Barton? I coulda shot you."

It had not yet registered with the occupant of the bed that Barton was only partially clad. The man laid the gun back down and brushed a hank of stringy black hair out of his eyes. He swung his stockinged feet over the side of the bed and inserted his arms through the loops of suspenders that lay in tired circles on the canvas bedding.

From a tin can on the floor the man withdrew a crooked black cigar. He lit the cheroot and drew a long drag before turning his head sideways to regard Barton.

"What happened to you?" he asked.

Barton explained the mishap in the saloon that had resulted in the loss of his clothing and his money belt. "Moffat, I need you to fetch my trunk from the Eagle and bring it here," he concluded.

"Only the trunk?" asked the large man with the greasy dark hair.

"No, the trunk *first*," Barton explained, "so I can dress properly to reserve our passage upriver on the morning steamer. After you retrieve the money belt from that miner who did me in, we'll want a sudden change of scenery, I think."

Outside the Eagle Saloon the street was dark. Fog broke from its tether on the knobby hills and drifted through the streets. The noise of raucous laughter echoed out of the tavern, and occasionally a miner, having exhausted his last pinch of dust, would stagger out and wander up the street.

Moffat stood leaning against the corner of the Epic Fire Company #1 building. He was smoking another cheroot and casually flicking the ashes onto the board sidewalk. He glanced up as each departing customer left the Eagle, but each time the features and dress were not those he had been instructed to single out.

At two A.M. he considered going back in to make sure the man he sought was still playing faro. Moffat decided against it for the time being. He had been noticed enough when collecting Barton's trunk, and he didn't want to stir up any suspicion.

Fifteen minutes later his patience was rewarded. The miner Barton had described to Moffat stepped out of the Eagle and paused before setting off, as if obligingly allowing Moffat to confirm his identity.

Moffat saw the man pat his belly. Undoubtedly it was not dinner that the man's gesture showed appreciation for, but rather Barton's money belt.

Moffat fingered the coil of rope in his coat pocket. The man took a deep breath of the cool air and then elected to walk up the street away from Moffat. Moffat began to follow him, in no hurry to close the gap until they were both well away from the entrance to the Eagle.

A short distance up the hill the fog closed in to darken the night even further and muffle the sounds of gambling and revelry. *Now*, Moffat thought, lengthening his stride to overtake the miner.

Moffat was five paces behind, then four, then three. His right hand started to produce the rope, and then a board creaked underfoot.

The miner whirled around and bent to place his hand on the knife handle protruding from his boot top. "Who's there?" he demanded.

Moffat dropped the half-drawn rope back into his pocket. He spread his hands wide in a gesture of harmlessness, and walked slowly up to stand in front of the man he had been following.

"Please, sir," he whined, "can you spare a bit for a poor, starving man what ain't eat for two days?"

The miner stood up, drawing his knife from its sheath as he did so. He patted the flat of the blade against the palm of his hand as he replied, "You don't look like you've missed too many meals yet. Be off with you."

Moffat ducked his head and backed away one step, then another. Just at the moment when it seemed he would turn to go, he stretched out his left arm and pointed over the miner's shoulder.

"Look there! Another big blaze is breaking out!"

The miner turned to look and swung the knife around away from Moffat. This was all the opportunity Moffat needed. He drew the coil of rope and quickly shook it out, holding one end in each hand. Moffat stepped up behind the prospector, and before the man could turn around again, had flipped the rope over his head and around his neck. The attacker crossed his hands and began pulling with all his strength, tightening the loop of hemp.

The victim tried to turn to face his attacker, but Moffat put his knee in the man's back and kept him tightly crushed against the rope.

The prospector slashed backward with the knife, but Moffat saw the blows coming and swung his victim around in a small circle. The blade flashed down once and then again; on a third missed stab, it fell from the miner's hand.

The prospector's fingers went up to his throat, attempting to get a grip under the coarse fibers to pull it away from his neck. His nails scrabbled on the line, his body beginning to stumble awkwardly as his brain clouded.

The miner's eyes protruded from his head. He tried to scream for help, but could not make any sound pass his tortured throat. The pull backward on the rope and the push forward in the small of his back made him feel as if he were breaking in two.

He was almost right. Moffat twitched the rope sideways with a sudden jerk of both hands, and a cracking noise like the sound of a tree branch breaking under a load of snow echoed up the deserted street. The prospector's body slumped to the boardwalk. His tongue protruded from his lips and his dead eyes still bulged from their sockets. This was one gambling miner who would never catch Barton cheating again.

Moffat looked up and down the deserted street. Then, reaching into the man's shirt, he removed Barton's money belt with a yank that rolled the corpse over. The dead man came to rest face down in the muddy San Francisco street, while Moffat strolled away, whistling to himself.

CHAPTER 6

Strawfoot, David, and Keo met up at *Bernice*'s dock as planned. They had a beautiful clear morning to cross the bay and an onshore breeze to push Keo's lobster-claw shaped sail. All in all, it would have been perfect, if David hadn't had such an abominable headache.

Christened the *Gold Seeker* by Strawfoot, who had romance in his blood but no seamanship, the little whaleboat bounced across San Francisco Bay. On the way they passed other Argonauts in all manner of crafts, including homemade rafts that spun and turned with each whim of the current. The men aboard these and other frail-looking boats paddled mightily with their makeshift oars. David could tell by their irrepressible grins that they were on course for the gold fields and even pleased with their progress.

They passed the first night at the port of Benecia. A United States customs official briefly examined their cargo and asked a couple of questions about their origin, destination, and purpose. He nodded wearily as if to say, "I knew that already," when they relayed their intent to prospect for gold. He passed them through with a tired wave of his hand and turned instead to a more thorough search of the cargo vessel *Milwaukee*.

The next day found them entering the Sacramento

River, and the propelling breeze failed them. Over Strawfoot's protests that he had been hornswoggled, they took turns hiking along the shore with a length of cable. The two men on board the *Gold Seeker* would row while the one on shore would wrap the cable around a tree trunk and pull for all he was worth. In this way they made substantial, if painful, progress.

Hiking through the muck and tule marshes and enveloped in a swarm of mosquitoes, David was reminded of the rain forests of his home island. *Except*, he thought to himself, *the mosquitoes at home were never this many or this big.*

The second night up the river they tied the whaleboat to an overhanging limb of an oak tree that jutted out over the waterway. David was so tired that he voted to eat cheese and crackers from their supplies and then turn in. The other two agreed, and soon all were fast asleep.

The following day went much the same, except that when daylight began to fail, there was no oak tree nearby. In fact, there was no tree of any size in sight. The tule bog that bordered that reach of river stretched uninterrupted for miles.

"We can't tie up to these reeds," complained David. "The current will break us loose for sure, and we'll be way downstream again by morning."

"Don't this here boat have an anchor or somethin'?" inquired Strawfoot, rubbing his neck.

"Whaleboat no need anchor," explained Keo. "Maybe we can find something."

He rummaged around in their store of goods and came up with a large cast-iron kettle. "Will work, yes?"

Cast-iron kettles just like this were used by the prospectors for all manner of duties. Strawfoot recounted for David how this pot would cook meals, wash clothes or render fat. David shuddered, remembering his recent experience around the try pots on the whale ship. Strawfoot concluded that he had never heard of one used as an anchor, but he didn't see why it wouldn't work.

They filled the kettle with mud and dumped it into the river. It dragged with the current for a moment or two, then successfully entangled itself in the matted tule roots. The three weary men settled down to sleep.

The next morning, David was the first to awaken. There had been a change in the level of the river during the night. That fact, coupled with some trick of the morning light, made the normally murky water extremely clear. Gazing around him and rubbing his eyes, David could follow the line of the rope connecting the boat to the kettle. The cast-iron pot was still faithfully holding the bow of the *Gold Seeker* into the current, even though the wash of the stream had cleaned the thick mud from its insides.

As David watched, a shaft of sunlight refracted into the kettle's dull black interior. Tiny glittering sparkles appeared, then disappeared, as a swirl of water obscured the bottom. David blinked hard and rubbed his eyes again. *Could it be?* he wondered. He had heard that the California streams were full of gold, but could it be literally true? He peered intently into the water. In a moment the river cleared, and immediately the inside of the kettle could be seen to glisten as if a tiny blacksmith were plying his trade and showering sparks around.

David's first few pulls drew the boat up to the anchor, but failed to break it free of the bottom. He called for help, and Keo began heaving on the rope as well. David excitedly explained about the flashes in the kettle, how it glinted just like gold, and how fortunate they were to have anchored in that spot.

Keo caught the excitement that David was generating. He leaned over the rail of the boat to grasp the handle of the kettle as it broke the surface, and with a mighty heave pulled it into the boat. Bucketfuls of water splashed over both David and Keo, spreading a stream of tiny, metallic flecks across the whaleboat's decking.

"Save it, save it!" shouted David. "Don't let those little flakes get away!"

Tiny particles were hastily gathered up. Keo transferred the little fragments from the tip of his right forefinger to the palm of his meaty left hand.

"Maybe cast iron attracts gold or something," spouted David. "Maybe we've found a secret method— or else just a real rich spot!"

"Or else two pair of new boots with greenhorn prospectors in 'em."

In his excitement, David hadn't noticed that Strawfoot had taken no part in gathering up the glittering particles. Now David turned to see the bearded man standing in the stern of the boat with his arms folded and his head cocked to the side.

Completely misunderstanding Strawfoot's meaning, David hurried to explain. "We weren't going to keep this gold separate. Honest, we were going to share everything we found. We were just hurrying because we got excited and didn't want to miss one little speck of this gold."

"Gold?" the prospector repeated. "I don't see no gold."

"But . . . but . . . right here," stammered David. "See how it shines?"

"Shade it in your hand," suggested Strawfoot. "Is it still gold color?"

"No," responded Keo, "is like black sand."

"Try and bite it," the prospector suggested to David. "And you," he said to Keo, "hammer it with somethin'."

They reported that it was gritty like sand and shattered when hammered. Strawfoot explained that real gold was soft when bitten, soft enough to hammer flat without shattering.

"But what is this stuff if it's not gold?" demanded David.

"I disremember what it's called for real," replied Strawfoot, "but it flakes out of the granite rocks up in the mountains. Most folks calls it 'fool's gold.'"

David and Keo looked at each other's wet clothes and the eager way they clutched the tiny fragments of worthless rock, and both began to laugh. "Pretty well named for such as us, isn't it, Keo?" said David, brushing his hands off on the seat of his trousers.

"You bet," responded the Hawaiian. "Maybe better we rename this boat LōLō."

"What's that mean?" asked Strawfoot.

"He says," answered David, "we should call it the *Stupid*."

———

Two more days of travel upriver brought the three partners to the confluence of the American and Sacramento rivers and to the settlement named for the latter.

"When I first come by here, they weren't but a half-rotted boat fetched up on the bank yonder and a tent store for a tradin' post. Now look at it." With a sweep of his arm, Strawfoot indicated the sprawling expanse of

Sacramento. Three sailing ships and a number of smaller craft were tied up to the wharf. A commercial district of shops and warehouses lined the docks. David could see that the buildings became simpler and shabbier as one looked farther inland. Just past the town on some cleared land nearby were acres and acres of tents, their occupants busily engaged in loading and unloading wagons.

"Where did all these people come from?" asked David. "We didn't see that many on the river."

"Bunch of these folks come here overland," explained Strawfoot. "Crossed the prairies and the Rockies and the deserts and the Sierras, and here they is." He added with an uncharacteristic note of surprise, "And they's lots more than when I was here last, too."

Strawfoot explained that they would have to go ashore here. Even though they could travel farther by river, this was the last opportunity to trade the whaleboat for overland transportation, namely mules. David reflected that he was sorry to part with the *Gold Seeker*, but the change meant that his voyaging had finally come to an end. Thousands of miles of water now lay between him and his home, but any regret was lost in his realization that only a few more miles stood between him and gold.

They pulled ashore past the wharf on a muddy bank near a solitary water oak some sixty feet tall. The riverbank rose to a plain twenty acres in expanse, crisscrossed by every conceivable wheeled, hoofed, and footed conveyance—men and their trappings off in the pursuit of wealth.

David saw a man pushing a wheelbarrow on which rested a chicken coop. The red rooster caged in the coop loudly proclaimed his independence and noisily challenged all comers to dispute his superiority. A team of six oxen pulling a high box freight wagon crossed the wheelbarrow's path by way of no discernible road. Around the base of the oak tree a string of mules were tethered, tended by a Mexican muleskinner wearing a serape and leather moccasins with leggings that reached up to his thighs.

A man galloping by on horseback scattered a disorganized group of miners who were walking across the muddy plain. David stared at the view—not because of the confusion, but because something seemed missing. What could possibly have been left out of a setting already so jumbled with men and their belongings? Then it struck him: there were no women anywhere in sight. It could have been a street scene at the waterfront of any number of busy port cities, except that Sacramento had no women at all. David wondered if the absence of female influence made men coarser and less civilized; then he mocked himself for unconsciously echoing one of his father's sermons.

Satisfied that he had resolved the mystery of what seemed wrong with Sacramento, David leaped ashore and plunged one of their crowbars into the clay bank, then tied the whaleboat securely.

Two hours later, Keo, David, and Strawfoot were headed upriver again, walking and leading a pair of mules. Strawfoot had successfully traded the whaleboat to one of Captain Sutter's lieutenants, and the supplies were loaded in short order.

As they traveled eastward, David noted the change of both scenery and climate. The low, marshy grassland gave way to foothills of oak trees, and the summer heat became drier.

"Strawfoot," David asked at one of their rest stops, "all this way you've just called your claim 'the diggins.' Does it have a name?"

Strawfoot gave a sideways glance at Keo, then allowed his gaze to rest on David, as if deciding whether or not to reply. Finally he launched in. "Well, it were mostly always called Old Dry Diggin's on accounta the first strikes was found up a ways from the creek. We had to carry the paydirt down to the stream to pan it, you see."

Strawfoot stopped, as if hoping that this account was satisfactory. David prompted him to continue by asking, "You say it *was* called that. What's it called now?"

The reply, when it came, was much lower in volume than Strawfoot's usual boisterous conversation. David leaned over toward the miner and caught the reply clearly: "Hangtown."

David rocked back upright, more startled by Strawfoot's dramatic manner than by the name itself. "Why did you hesitate to tell us?" he asked.

Strawfoot drew a deep breath and sighed heavily before continuing. When he did, it was in the same subdued tone. "Just after the turn of this year, three men was hanged up in the diggin's. They was part of a gang of five what had robbed a man and got caught."

"They were hanged for robbing?" interrupted David. Strawfoot waved his hand for silence and continued. "No, they was whipped for that. But whilst they was bein' lashed, three was recognized as having kilt a man up Stanislaus River way."

Strawfoot proceeded to explain that over a hundred

miners formed themselves into a jury and convicted the three in the space of half an hour. He recalled that a man named Buffum, a former Army lieutenant, was the only man to speak against the lynch law.

"But twarn't no use. Buffum was told to shut up or he'd be hanged, too. The boys was all likkered up, and nothin' would satisfy them, exceptin' . . ."

Strawfoot shook his head sadly and wiped his forehead with a red bandana.

David could sense how deeply painful this account was for Strawfoot, so he tried to sum up by noting, "But they had a fair trial, right? Only one man took their part? And nothing they could say would prove their innocence? Seems to me your miners taught a harsh, but correct, lesson."

Strawfoot stared into David's eyes with the look of a haunted man. It made David shudder, and the icy trickle of fear down his back made him stammer, "They were guilty, weren't they? Did they beg for mercy?"

Strawfoot's eyes looked through David to some recollection only he could see, but from which he could not turn away. "No, they didn't beg for mercy; they didn't speak no English, an' they couldn't even understand what they was charged with!"

Beside David, Keo exhaled a long breath through pursed lips, making a whistling, sighing sound. Very gently the big Hawaiian asked, "You vote for their death, too?"

Strawfoot nodded slowly and added, "An' when Buffum said that he would interpret, them bein' French an' him knowin' the language, I—me, Strawfoot—I shook a busted bottle in his face and told him to keep still or I'd cut his tongue out."

David unconsciously backed up two steps from the miner's side. The prospector noticed the unspoken reproof and added, "I sobered up next day and kept to myself ever since, minin' all alone. I got so lonesome, I went to Frisco for a spree. I figgered on pickin' some new partners, and then you come along. I didn't figger you for foreign till I saw Keo there. By then I didn't know what to say. See, I liked you right off. Anyways," he concluded sadly, "I guess you can make up your minds about me now."

David couldn't think of anything to say. He knew he'd never be so craven as to send men to their deaths without a word for their side. In his mind David cast himself as Buffum, the gallant, if unsuccessful, voice of reason. David watched with surprise as Keo moved toward the miner and put his bronzed arm around the prospector's shoulders.

"You feel grief for your part, yes?" David heard Keo ask. At Strawfoot's short bob of his head in agreement, Keo continued, "You Christian man? You know Jesus?" Again the brief nod. "Jesus speak no word to save Him from cross when all bad men say for Him to die. But He ask Father God not to crush them for killing His Son. You think maybe God forgive for Jesus, maybe God forgive you too?"

This was more than David could stand to hear. An ignorant native sailor was speaking words of redemption and forgiveness learned from David's father. And this bearded miner was actually responding, visibly brightening! David stalked off to be by himself for a while.

Later on, Keo approached David to report that Strawfoot was feeling much better and was ready to proceed. "Do you believe all that Bible story stuff you were handing him?" quizzed David gruffly.

"Kawika," responded the harpooner firmly. "I tell Strawfoot how God in his heart already forgive all his sins more than just one which make him so sad. I tell him God forgive me for worshiping stone gods in dark time." Keo stopped and looked thoughtfully at David, "He ready forgive you too, Kawika."

"Forgive me?" snorted David. "I don't need forgiveness. I haven't done anything wrong."

David's first glimpse of Hangtown was not what he expected—or, rather, more than he expected. The trail crested a low rise topped with pine trees, and suddenly the town lay immediately below him, nestled in a bowl-shaped depression. From the ridge he could count over forty buildings, and saw smoke rising from other chimneys hidden around a curve of the hill.

He turned to Strawfoot to ask if this was the right place, since it seemed so much bigger than the one he had described. Strawfoot responded that it had, in fact, changed a great deal since his departure. " 'Bout doubled, I figger."

For all its size, Hangtown did not seem overly busy or crowded with people. The prospector explained that the population of miners was spread up and down the creek working their claims until nightfall brought them to town.

"When I first seen the place," Strawfoot continued, "there wasn't but two log buildings hereabout. Everything else was tents and wickiups."

"When do we start mining gold?" asked David, unconsciously rubbing his hands together in anticipation.

"Hold your horses. My place is just upstream a ways. We'll go unload our gear and maybe dig a bit before dark."

The procession of three tired men and two very weary mules picked up their pace in expectation of arriving at camp. They skirted the edge of Hangtown by hiking around the rim of the valley, because this was a faster approach to Strawfoot's claim.

"It's just through this gap here," said Strawfoot, pointing to where the path led between granite boulders. In his excitement to be home he raced ahead of the others.

When he reached the space between the rocks where the path began to descend toward the creek, he stopped stock still. David saw him stiffen, almost as if he had been slapped in the face. David and Keo hurried up to stand beside him.

"My cabin's gone," the miner said in a harsh croak. "It were just yonder by that pinyon tree. Now there's three tents there."

"And my claim!" he shouted, waving his arms. "Somebody has gone and wingdammed the creek and backed it up over my bar." With that he took off at a run down the hill toward the stream, all thought of partners, mules, and supplies left behind.

David and Keo followed him down the path to stand beside the pinyon pine. Twenty Chinese miners were working beside the stream. Some were digging down to the bedrock in the stream bed uncovered when the wing-dam diverted the water. Others were transporting the sand and gravel to a long tom set up beside the stream, while still others were walking along beside the wooden frame, turning the muddy contents with shovels. A few glanced up at the new arrivals, but none left off working.

Presently a tall man, dressed like all the rest in high boots and baggy pants, but white and armed with an unmistakable air of authority, came over to where they stood.

"Can I help you men?" he asked. "Are you looking for work?"

"Work!" exploded Strawfoot. "I'm looking for my claim! And while we're about it, where'd my cabin get off to? Who are you, anyway?"

The man seemed unruffled by the flurry of questions. He scanned Strawfoot up and down and spared a glance or two for David and Keo before remarking, "You must be Strawfoot. We heard you were dead, but obviously it isn't true."

Strawfoot snorted, a sound David thought closely resembled a bull in a dangerous mood. "No, I ain't dead! Not by a long shot. But some others 'round here may be right soon if I don't hear why all these folks are messin' around my claim!"

"Calm down, Mr. Strawfoot. My name is Foster. I'm the foreman here with the Amalgamated Mining Company."

"The what? I've never heard tell of your outfit. Where do you get off damming the creek and covering up another man's claim?"

"Your claim's played out, Mr. Strawfoot. We took every foot of gravel off and swept the bedrock of your claim before we diverted the river. We put up your gold in a jar—in case your heirs turned up to claim it."

"All played out," puffed Strawfoot, suddenly deflated like a bellows with a ripped out seam. "But I took thousands out of that claim."

"I've heard that. By sheerest good fortune you hit the only pocket on your stretch. Two feet either way, and there was nothing. We scraped up every flake we could find, but it didn't amount to more than, oh, another pound or so."

"All played out?" Strawfoot repeated, clearly struggling with the thought of how much gold he'd blown on his spree in Frisco.

"For what it's worth," Foster continued, "you can have your claim back soon. We've about exhausted the stream bed here also, so you can tear down the wingdam if you've a mind to."

"What about his cabin?" asked David, with the sinking feeling that his dream of instant wealth had taken wings and flown away.

"That cabin, I'm sorry to say, burned down. I don't know what possessions you may have lost, but we can provide you with a tent to use."

"Is it your company that's made the town grow so?" inquired David.

Foster explained that Hangtown's growth was mainly due to its place on one of the main routes over the Sierras from the East. "Ever since the passes cleared, they have been coming—first by the tens, but lately by the hundreds. All gold seekers in search of El Dorado. Well, they'll need to search elsewhere. We're about done here, except for fluming the river to use it in a dry canyon that shows promise. A company of Chinese is going to buy this stretch—more fools they. Now I've got to get back to work. Good day to you, gentlemen."

"What'll we do now?" said David to Keo, ignoring Strawfoot. The miner was staring so grimly over the scene in front of him that David was almost afraid to interrupt his thoughts.

"Maybe we can work for these folks for a time," commented Keo. "They hire Chinese, so maybe they take Kanaka and haole."

That comment got a rise out of Strawfoot. Bristling all over he declared, "Work for these Amal Gee Mates? Not on your tintype. I'd ruther be shot in the rear with a pint of hornets! I found this here claim, didn't I? I'll just find another one!"

CHAPTER 7

The three partners crossed a high ridge northeast of Hangtown and struck out for what they hoped would be unexplored territory, rich with gold. For two days they travelled, rejecting location after location because of the astounding number of other prospectors already working claims. At last they reached an expanse of steep canyons covered in fir trees, and Strawfoot declared it was time to begin prospecting.

At the first of these stops Strawfoot directed David and Keo to dig out a pile of gravel from the foot of a massive boulder. This rock sometimes lay in the path of the creek, but the lowered water level had left it dry. Strawfoot explained that when the flood water washed against the rock and turned the current to the side, pockets in the bank could trap gold washed down from farther up.

They dug down until Strawfoot was satisfied they were below the surface soil. Taking a pan and a shovelful of earth from the hole, he squatted beside the stream and began swirling the dirt away.

David and Keo stood looking over his shoulder. David held his breath with anticipation. He saw the miner squint his eyes, frown, purse his lips and stare off into the distance.

"What is it?" asked David eagerly, "Is there gold? Not fool's gold, I hope."

"Why shore, it's real enough," began Strawfoot, when his explanation was cut short by David almost knocking the pan from his hand.

"Show me!" demanded David. "These flakes here? Is this gold?"

Strawfoot straightened up and stretched his back and legs. "Shore am out of practice for setting by a pan all day," he remarked.

"Why aren't you more excited?" questioned David. "You said it *is* gold?"

"Oh there's gold, right enough. I count eight specks in this here pan."

"Eight specks—is that good?"

"Not less'n you want to eat beans the rest of your life. I calculate if we worked here from sunup to sunset, we might make ten dollars a day."

"But that's not enough to feed the three of us!" David cried, shocked at the news. "What do we do now?"

"That's why they call it prospecting," replied Strawfoot. "We've gotta keep looking somewheres else."

Two more days passed this way. Strawfoot would lead them to a likely spot, where they dug a test hole. A few swirls of the pan, and the contents would be dumped back into the creek, the few tiny flakes left to lure other gold seekers.

Finally Strawfoot's examination of the gold pan lasted longer than usual. Weary from a day of tramping over steep hillsides and climbing in and out of narrow ravines, David hardly paid any attention. His thoughts were wandering back to San Francisco, to the fancy hotels and sumptuous meals that gold could provide.

Keo, his usual stoic self, was watching closer than David. "Is good color?" he asked, combining his Hawaiian inflection with prospector jargon.

"Yup, I'm satisfied," announced Strawfoot.

This startled David out of his daydream. "You mean we've struck it? This is a worthwhile spot?"

"See for yourself," responded Strawfoot, extending the pan toward David.

The ridge where the slanted side of the pan met the bottom was a solid line of gold flakes around half of the circumference. In the center of the curve was the real prize: a nugget the size of the last joint of David's little finger.

"What do you figure? I mean, how much can we make here? A day, I mean?"

"Well," began Strawfoot, pulling his beard into a bushy handful. "If this pan's showing holds good for this stretch of creek bed, we can do, say, a hundred dollars a day betwixt us."

"Three thousand a month!" exclaimed David. "What are we waiting for?" and he began attacking the sandbar with as much enthusiasm as if he'd been starving and a roast pig lay underneath the ground.

"Simmer down," advised Strawfoot. "Now that we've located, we'll fix us a proper camp. I'm tired of sleepin' in a bedroll with no tent between me an' the crawly critters. Plus, I got to knock together that rocker we been carryin', so we can get serious. Here," he added, handing David the nugget from the pan. "Keep this for good luck." David accepted the gold lump and tucked it into his shirt pocket, buttoning the flap down to keep it safe.

By the following afternoon they had "got serious."

All three attacked the stream bed until paydirt was uncovered and a pile of it dug out with pick and shovel. Keo kept the wooden box called a rocker in motion, swirling the water around the pailful of earth David dumped in the top. David followed up the load of dirt by carrying pail after pail of water to be added to the mixture. Strawfoot collected the gold flakes and a few nuggets from the riffle bars in the rocker's insides and processed the fine sand and gold with his pan.

The routine produced $120 worth of gold their first day. David was elated. He was really a prospector now, and on his way to being rich. Amazingly, even after all the calluses he'd acquired scrubbing the decks of the *Crystal*, David's hands still found new places to blister. He grimaced as the handles of the heavy pails of water cut into his fingers, but he was satisfied that when he escaped from this pain, he would be wealthy.

The next day's work produced $100, and the day after, $90. Each evening the three would work until dark, then gather around the lamp for a weighing process that became a solemn ceremony. Strawfoot would unpack a pan balance and a set of brass weights and tally up the day's results. The flake gold was poured into a leather pouch and the pouch tucked beneath the bedrolls. Lumps of gold were divided up among the three men, each man taking turns selecting until all were gone. David rarely thought of home any more; he went to bed each night exhausted, but happy, thinking of all his new-found wealth could buy.

A shaft of sunlight arcing through the tent flap struck David in the eyes. On one side of him, Keo was sleeping peacefully, while on the other, Strawfoot sounded like he was sawing timber for a few thousand rockers.

Through the opening David could see the creek and a pile of their tools. The trunk of a fallen cedar lay partly in the stream, and the uphill side was covered in a layer of ladybugs. As David watched, one detached itself from the mass and flew almost directly toward the tent, striking the canvas with a tiny but audible thump.

What a peaceful morning, thought David. *It reminds me of Sunday mornings back home, before Father would yell at me to hurry up or I'd be late for service.*

David wondered drowsily why the morning seemed so peaceful. His brain turned this thought over while he watched a blue jay swoop down from a redwood to land on a rock that was part of their cooking ring.

Something finally clicked and he sat up, saying out loud, "Hey, why are we sleeping so late?" Strawfoot always got them up in the gray light, before dawn. Now it was full light and still the prospector let them sleep.

Strawfoot mumbled, "Sabbath. Day of rest," and turned over again.

"But say," objected David, "what about the gold?"

"Still be there tomorrow," breathed the miner through his whiskers.

"But it's my day to have first choice of the nuggets, and I feel lucky today," objected David.

"You can have your turn tomorrow," explained the prospector, now fully awake. "Me and Keo talked this over after you'd already dropped off last night. We want to give the Almighty his due, so we figger on reading some scripture verses and bein' grateful for a day of rest."

David turned over to find Keo also awake and

propped on one elbow regarding him with liquid brown eyes. "Is Lord's Day, Kawika. He let us keep gold, we let Him keep one day. Long time whale ship no different Sabbath Day from other day. Is good idea."

"Well I don't think it's such a good idea. You two lie around camp if you want to, but I'm going to run some pans, if nothing else. And I'm going to keep what I find, too."

"Okay Kawika, you go. Maybe get out of camp do you good. God show His work all around here," added Keo, extending his broad palm toward the sunlit creekside. "Maybe you talk to Him some, too."

———

David took off away from camp to prospect. He rationalized that he didn't want to make Keo and Strawfoot feel bad because he was working and they were having a day of rest. The truth was, he felt uncomfortable staying in camp when they were reading from the Bible. An unnamed irritation came over him—they believed him to be in the wrong, even though no one had tried to force anything on him. He threw the shovel he was carrying into a sand bar with more force than was necessary.

David dug beside the stream and turned a few pans of gravel in the clear water, but found no color. He found himself unable to concentrate on what he was doing and reproved himself for being stupid. How much concentration did it take to dig a hole?

In any case, he trudged on upstream, trying to recall all the signs that Strawfoot had suggested looking for.

Another sandbar, another two feet of gravel, and the same result. Digging down to bedrock seemed like too much work. After all, David felt that the gold should be calling to him, practically jumping into his pan.

Something was calling to him—not audibly, but persistently, in his head. For the third time he stopped to try to determine what was bothering him. As he paused to consider this elusive annoyance, he noticed that he had dug his test hole too near the course of the stream and the hole was filling with water. Throwing his pan down in disgust, David settled on this interruption as a good excuse to lean against a nearby boulder and think.

Sunday morning in the mountains of the Sierra Nevada. He squinted up at the sun shining down through the branches of a willow tree growing across the stream. It was about ten o'clock, he judged. Just the time at home when his father would be ringing the handbell that called his flock to worship.

David closed his eyes and let the warm sunshine bathe his face. It wasn't nearly as intense as the sun would have been at home. On the other hand, the breeze in this Sierra canyon was clean, but it carried none of the heady sweet aroma of the Ilima and Pikake blossoms that grew outside his bedroom window.

When the islanders decorated the church altar with fragrant bouquets, David's father would always make a point to draw a deep breath of jasmine or the scent of gardenias, then spread his arms as if to embrace the whole congregation. He would thank those who had brought the flowers for blessing the very air with their gift, and then remind them that the fragrance of the blossoms was like the enjoyment God receives from the prayers of His people.

David's eyes popped open with a snap. They were

praying for him! He knew it with a certainty, and in that same instant understood what had been nagging him all morning. It was Sunday morning, and they were praying for him!

David looked at the gold pan lying at his feet and put a hand to his buttoned shirt pocket to touch the gold nugget there. *If they only knew how little I need their prayers,* he thought. *I'm well, getting rich and having an adventure. In their entire lives they'll never be twenty miles from the village where they were born.*

David stretched—an expansive, relaxed stretch. He was relieved to have figured out what had been on his mind. *Let them pray for me,* he thought, *even if I don't need it.*

David decided to relax a moment longer there on the warm slab of granite. He put his hands behind his head and began to lie down on the rock. Halfway down he stopped and turned over to brush the pine needles and ladybugs from his wilderness bench. Mid-motion, he froze.

Right behind him, also taking advantage of the morning sun, was a coiled snake. David sat up slowly, inspecting the resting reptile with curiosity but no fear. Hawaii had no native snakes, and David saw no reason to be afraid of this one that was so amiably sharing the boulder. Strawfoot had warned David and Keo about the poisonous snakes called rattlers that inhabit these mountains, but he had told them about their warning rattle and their belligerent striking. This snake hadn't offered to do either. It was small, dark brown in color. Its scales were dull and drab, and it had a squat, unattractive head.

As David watched, the snake tested the air with quick

pulses of its forked tongue. The reptile moved its head from side to side as though looking for something; although at two feet away, David was the only thing that could possibly be in sight. He was stretching out his hand to touch it when he heard the music.

Very faint, echoing off the canyon walls, was the sound of singing. This was no church music; David could hear snatches of lyrics like *My dearest Sally . . . I'll go to Californy . . . and she threw a dozen in*! A mining camp, without a doubt—and just one canyon over, by the sound of it.

David decided he had dug enough dirt for one week; he would hike on over to that camp and see what it was like. He glanced back toward the snake, but in the moment when his attention had shifted, so had the serpent. He caught just a quick glimpse of its tail as it disappeared down a hole. *That's strange*, David puzzled. *Those little buttons sure look like I'd expect rattles to look.* Shrugging, he gathered up his pan and shovel and set out to hike over the hill.

As David crossed the ridge line and began to descend the canyon on the other side, the music grew louder and the words more distinct. He heard a mixture of voices, some good and some bad, some old and some young, but none female. They were singing, "I fed him last at Chimney Rock, that's where the grass gave out; I'm proud to tell we stood it well along the Truckee route. . . ."

Apparently Sally was a popular name for the girl left behind, for the next song also had a Sally handing out advice: "Here take the laud'num with you Sam, to check the diaree." It didn't seem that any of these travelers needed the mentioned remedy, for all were dancing in a lively manner. They would have benefited from the presence of Sally and her sisters; however, the dancers were all male. Some partners wore bandanas tied to their arms, but in the stomping and whirling, it was impossible to tell who was leading anyway.

David approached the outskirts of the ruckus and leaned his shovel and pan against a tree. He found a tall, bald man who was neither dancing, singing, nor playing fiddle or banjo. The bald man, who *was* smiling and tapping his foot in time to the music, looked over at David as he arrived. "Welcome, stranger. Where are you from?"

"My friends and I have a claim downstream on the next creek over," David answered. "I followed the music, and here I am."

"Yessir, good for what ails you. Dancing and music and kicking up your heels. This is the Washington Company, son. We've been four months on the way here from Michigan. Lost half our stock before we ever saw the South Pass of the Rockies and had more stolen by Digger Indians. We buried a few of the company, too. Some from cholera back in Missouri, and one just about your age, just last week."

Startled by this flood of words from a complete stranger, it took David a moment to realize that the pause after the last statement showed the expectation of a question.

"Um, uh, what did he die of?" asked David, finally catching on.

"A wagon fell on him. We were hoisting our equipment up by ropes, just like it says to do in *Hasting's Guidebook*, when a rope broke and he couldn't get out of the way in time. But we're here now," the man continued, "and we aim to celebrate before we go to mining."

"Did you say you had a *guidebook*?" asked David incredulously.

"You bet. Lansford Hastings. Of course, he had some of the landmarks wrong, but on the whole his was better than the others."

"The others? Is there a regular business in guide-books?"

"You can say that again! And not surprising, either; I think the whole country's coming west. There were times when we could see a line of wagons stretching to the horizon in both directions. Just look around you," offered the man. "We've only been here two days and we've started to build cabins and a dam to divert water from the creek bed. We've got carpenters, engineers, blacksmiths. Why, we'll be a regular settlement in no time at all."

The man gestured toward a tent building that stretched along one side of the dance floor. "That's our store. Already open for business."

"You mean you brought trade goods all the way across the continent?" David was clearly ready to be impressed.

The man looked momentarily embarrassed. "Actually, most of the stuff got thrown out coming across. But—" He paused for effect. "We do have whiskey. Twenty-five cents a glass."

Several samples of trade goods later, David made his way back across the ridge to camp. He explained to Kco and Strawfoot about the nearness of the other camp and talked at great length about the vast numbers of miners, who were apparently just beginning to arrive.

Strawfoot seemed to shrug off the news as being of no concern. "There's still plenty for everybody," he said, "and plenty more places to look, too."

Their claim continued to pay well enough for several

weeks. David still left camp on Sundays, but he did no prospecting and he took no long walks just to think. Instead, he went directly to the neighboring mining camp, now big enough to be called a settlement. David showed some luck at the faro tables, but he was quick to notice that the man acting as the "bank" was the only sure winner.

Members of the Washington Company drifted over to the canyon where Keo, Strawfoot, and David were working. Their camp had proposed some rules for fair play, they said, and they considered the side stream as part of the same mining territory.

David listened as the rules were explained. Each miner's claim was to be limited to ten yards of stream frontage. No man could hold more than one claim, and work had to be done at least one day out of seven for the claim to be valid.

There was no discussion of these rules, nor were the three partners asked for their opinion. Their "company" was allowed one additional claim for the right of discovery, but that was it. Soon a hundred miners were working up and down the creek where once only Strawfoot's solitary tent had stood. Strawfoot seemed to think that the rules were just and proper, but David frowned and turned surly whenever a prospector announced a rich find or displayed an especially large nugget.

Eventually the return dropped off considerably. They were processing larger amounts of gravel each day, but finding less gold. When their take had fallen below thirty-five dollars for three weeks in a row, they decided it was time for a change. David felt as if he had personally dug up every rock on half a mile of stream, so he had no regrets about moving on.

They decided to continue moving upriver. Strawfoot told them about the "mother lode," a ledge of pure gold somewhere in the mountains that was supposedly the source of all the flakes, grains, and nuggets found in the streams.

Despite Strawfoot's sense that there was "plenty for everyone," for several days they saw no opportunity to test a likely spot, for every one they came to was already staked. They passed one stretch of creek where all the miners were from Mexico and spoke only Spanish. Another day brought them to another area populated by Chinese immigrants. The Chinese were working a bar already examined by other miners and rejected as showing too little promise. But the "Celestials," as the Chinese were called, methodically sifted the sand so that not even the finest particle of gold escaped their search.

Obtaining supplies became increasingly difficult. Even walking as rapidly as possible, one man could not lead a mule down to the trading post, load up, and complete the trek back upcountry in less than three days. Sometimes it took even longer if the trading post was out of flour, bacon, or other essentials. The man hauling the freight wouldn't dare to leave before being resupplied, or the store might run out before he got back again.

Prices were outrageous. Flour sold for a dollar a pound, and eggs, when they could be had at all, for a dollar each. The level of gold dust in the partnership sack began to diminish instead of increase.

Finally the morning came when David, sleeping next to the wall of the tent, rolled over into it, shaking the canvas. A shower of ice crystals shattered down on his face and neck, waking him up instantly. He lay in the dark for a minute, trying to figure out what had happened, and discovered that his breath was condensing and freezing inside the tent. They would have to decide what to do, and soon. Clearly winter was not far away.

CHAPTER 8

"I say we head for town for the winter—Hangtown, at least, but Sacramento would be even better." David vigorously pushed for the three partners to get out of their mountain camp.

"If we skedaddle now while there's still another month of working weather, other folks will move in on our claim. Come spring, this whole stretch of country will be shoulder to shoulder with miners." Strawfoot was just as determined to stay, unaware that he was now arguing that there was *not* unlimited gold.

"Let's just sell this claim, then," responded David. "We're not making but an ounce a day, most days, sometimes less. Why don't we sell out, find some cozy spot to hole up, and prospect some other place in spring?"

"Didn't you hear anything I said? There won't be anybody *buying* claims this close to winter, but they'll sure take over one that's been abandoned."

"Why don't we let them have it, then?" shrugged David. "If we stay here any longer we may have to winter over, and that doesn't appeal to me. What about you, Keo?"

Both miner and young man turned to the native for his opinion. Keo tugged on his bushy side whiskers in thought before replying. "I think Strawfoot is right, Ka-

103

wika. If we stay here now, others will be the ones leaving. Perhaps we better our claim. If we all work, we can have a fine cabin before snow comes. Then spring will find us already at work, not looking for a place."

"So that's how it is, eh Keo?" said David with a sneer.

"Why you sound so full with HuHū, so angry, Kawika? Did we not say if two agree, the third will say aye?"

"Did you know that you only speak Hawaiian when you're trying to convince me about something, Keo? Well, it won't work this time. I'm tired of being cold, I'm tired of working twelve hours a day just to get enough money to feed us. I'm tired of the lousy food, and I'm tired of both of you. That's it! It's all pau! Pau, Keo. Finished!"

"Now hold on a minute, Bollin," protested Strawfoot. "We said this partnership had to stay together till we come out of the hills. We need your share of the dust to have enough for supplies to see us through the winter, and we need another pair of hands to help build a cabin that's snug. You can't leave till we all do."

David turned to rummage through a knapsack. "I thought it might come to this," he announced. He pulled out the derringer taken from Barton back in Frisco, and calmly cocked the hammer. "Now weigh out my share, and let me get out of here."

"Do not do this, Kawika," begged Keo.

"You won't miss me," replied the young man. "You two can just go on having your prayer meetings without me like you were anyway. I'm through grubbing in the dirt." With that, David helped himself to a third of the gold, shouldered his knapsack, and turned to leave. "If you think I've taken out more than my share," he added, "remember that I let you keep both mules. I don't expect to need them again." Then he was gone.

It was only a rumor, brought to Honolulu by a whaling ship refitting for the season. A passenger from an unnamed schooner had been swept overboard and picked up by the whale ship *Crystal*. Those who heard the rumor, which had passed from ship to ship, were uncertain if the young passenger had been alive or dead when he was fished from the deep. Common sense dictated that he was dead.

But the heart of Kapono Bollin chose to believe that David was alive. *Here at last was hope!*

The warm Kona wind brought a perfect, drowsy stillness to the air, and yet the congregation of Kapono William Bollin was stirring this afternoon.

Clean woven mats were spread out beneath the trees. A pig had been killed and roasted to succulent perfection in a pit behind the church.

Sweet voices were raised in joyful hymns as the people gathered to feast one last time with their beloved teacher. Although the voices were light, hearts were heavy today. Many had grown to adulthood never knowing any other teacher but Kapono Bollin. What would they do without him?

"Why you want to go there, Kapono Bollin?" asked a tall, brown-skinned young man who had learned to read in the class of the *haole* preacher-man.

The pastor dipped his hand into a large calabash filled with poi. The curious brown eyes of the other villagers turned to consider Kapono Bollin as he answered.

"Many hearts have been won here." He spoke so softly

that all the others fell silent to hear him. "But I have lost my own son, and if he is still alive, I must find him."

The wife of Edward Hupeka frowned. "But California is such a terrible place, Kapono Bollin. Dangerous and wild. We hear there is no law there. No king. No God."

"I am not afraid," answered Kapono Bollin. "Hawaii was once a place with many gods and a king who sacrificed his people to idols. And yet we came here."

"But we were waiting to hear of Iesu," replied Hohu, a very old man whose tattooed body had once bowed down before the altars of human sacrifice. "We longed to hear the word of Iesu and true Aloha. *Ora loa ia Iesu! Endless life by Jesus!*"

"Yes," agreed another, "in California the white men do not wish to hear. They have run from the churches and the laws of the East."

Quietly Mary added, *"But perhaps David is there!"*

All eyes turned toward her. There was small hope of such a miracle. Only Mary and Kapono Bollin believed it could be so. And everyone knew they believed and hoped because they loved too much. They loved even though David had rejected them. Such love was a heavy burden.

"Dear Kapono Bollin." Old Emma Ipo put a gnarled hand on the arm of the preacher. "What if David is not? I am *Iuahine*—an old woman. When I was young my husband was killed in battle with King Kamehameha. They tell me, but I do not believe. Every day I look and wait. I bear his child—" She waved a hand toward her son at the far end of the mat. "I still believe my *kāne* not dead. I live in false hope for many year." She pursed her lips in thought. "Why you not stay here with us who have great aloha for you?"

The soul of William Bollin wrenched at the thought of leaving this place and these people after so long. He inhaled deeply and searched for the right words. "Once we were all lost, Emma, and the Good Shepherd came to find us." He frowned. "If David still lives, I must look for him."

"There are no churches in California. Maybe you will not come back, Kapono Bollin," said the young man sadly.

William Bollin answered in Hawaiian. *"Ku'u Kahu no Iesu!—The Lord my shepherd is.* I am not afraid."

They all understood. Kapono Bollin had no thought for his own safety. Everyone knew that Kapono Bollin did not care so much for dying since the day news had come that David was swept away. Perhaps that was the real reason he now wished to travel to such a terrible and wild land as California.

Much later that night, when the lamp in Kapono Bollin's house went out, the people still spoke of it among themselves as they cleaned up from the feast.

The elders of the village remembered what life had been before the missionaries had come. They had seen much. They had witnessed many miracles. *"Ka'a mau ke akua!"* declared the old man as he raised his tattooed arm. *"God moves in a mysterious way!* He sometimes leads men to walk where they do not wish to walk. In the end, sometimes men turn into the arms of Iesu. Sometimes they run from God and fall into the belly of old *Pele* who eats them with fire. Jesus is the Shepherd of our Kapono. Kapono Bollin is more safe on that narrow path with God than anywhere without God. As for us, we have only to pray. The rest is not for us to think on."

The people listened to the old man and felt much better. They sang softly as the moon climbed to a silver crescent above the village.

———

Barton shuffled the cards with an expert flourish and offered them to a small dark man seated at his left. After the cut of the cards, the gambler reassembled them in a neat pile. With a snapping sound audible over the clinking glasses and the hubbub of the saloon, he flicked over the first card.

"Ace of spades, gentlemen. A bad luck card already turned. Place your bets. Who feels lucky?" With a practiced forefinger he pushed one ball up the row beside the ace on the card counter.

Three other miners sat around the faro table with the little dark man. Moffat hovered behind them, a glass of whiskey in his hand. The four players studied the layout of the betting board, on which painted figures of each of the thirteen cards could be seen.

"Next card's the winner and then the loser, gentlemen. Court the one and avoid the other. Place your bets."

The short man wagered an ounce of dust on the queen, and the others made their selections. When the bets were down, Barton flipped over the cards in rapid succession. The first revealed was a ten on which no one had bet, the second the queen. Barton reached over and casually removed the small doeskin pouch of gold dust and smoothly deposited it in a box by his feet.

When Barton had moved the counters for the ten and queen, he announced, "Three down, gentlemen. Who can guess the order of the next two? Place your bets."

The play continued this way for thirty minutes or so,

with Barton paying off on an occasional lucky guess, but winning more often than not. Once he turned up a pair of jacks and another time two fives appeared; each time he accepted half the wagered amount as the house per-centage. When the deck was exhausted he declared, "Let's all take a break for drinks, gentlemen. Who's thirsty?"

While the players moved to the bar, Barton held a quiet conference with Moffat. "How'd we do?" asked the killer.

We're up about two hundred dollars on the night," replied the gambler. "All the luck is coming our way, too. I haven't had to pull a second so far. What have you heard? Anything interesting?"

"Nah. These miners don't give a rip about owning property. All they care about is their stretch of creekbed. You want me to put together a gang so we can push some of them out of the way?"

"Moffat, you have no subtlety at all," Barton growled. "Haven't you heard any griping about anything? Some complaint we can play to?"

"These rock-hoppers grouse about everything, but nothing that'll turn us a nickel. They're down on the cost of food, the price of shovels, the Chinks, the lousy whis-key, the greasers, the lack of women, the—"

"Hold it!" ordered Barton. "What did you say?"

"I said they're looking for camp floozies, but what—"

"No, before that. Never mind, Moffat. I need to think a little. Chinks and greasers, you say. Tomorrow we may need to travel to improve our knowledge. Come on, it's time to start the game again."

———

"I tell you it's the truth. Them Chinese can see at night! They ain't human, I tell you. Sifting through a ton of sand to find specks of gold as fine as flour dust," spouted a pot-bellied miner with red hair.

"But where's the harm in that?" needled Barton. "If they want to work harder or longer, shouldn't they be allowed to?"

"Friend, I can see you haven't been in this country for long. I hear tell there's a hundred million of them Celestials, and more coming all the time. Pretty soon they'll be spreading out all up and down this country, and then where'll we be?"

"And it ain't just the Chinks," asserted another miner, a skinny man with a bulbous nose and wandering Adam's apple. "You can't trust nobody what don't know good English. Why, how can you tell what they's thinking, if you can't even understand them when they talk? Greasers and them other Spanish talkers hang together pretty thick, too."

Barton let the conversation run on without pressing the issue further. He'd already gotten the information he sought: there was growing anti-foreign sentiment in the prospecting community. Of course, it was mostly confined to men who did more talking than prospecting and more complaining than working, but that suited Barton's purposes all the better.

All up and down the streams, the pressures of thousands of gold seekers competing for space was beginning to be felt. Already some prime locations were known to be in the hands of the Chinese, the Mexicans—even miners from Peru and Chile. *But,* Barton thought to himself, *not for long.*

David ambled down the trail toward Hangtown, whistling to himself. He carried a pound of gold dust and nearly another pound in nuggets. It wasn't a lot, but David knew what he would do to get more. He planned to buy a second-hand faro outfit and set himself up as a professional gambler.

He shook his head in derision as he passed knots of miners working along the streams, and laughed to himself when some hopeful prospector hiked by, eager to get to the diggings. His mind was occupied with thoughts of gambling halls, and hotels with real beds and decent food. He licked his lips at the memory of his last drink of whiskey, and pictured himself decked out in a new suit of clothes.

It's San Francisco for me, he mused. He expected to earn enough at each stage of his descent from the mountains to finance a move to the next larger and more elegant setting.

David stopped off in the tent saloon at Washington. He didn't intend to stay there long or to gamble with any of his precious stake of gold. Even though Washington had grown in size as predicted, it was still a ramshackle collection of tents and bark shelters and shanty hovels.

What he really wanted was a drink. He stepped up to the counter to discover that the tall, bald man he had met on previous visits to Washington was now tending bar.

"Well, if it isn't David Bollin, back from the wars. Where you been keeping yourself, Bollin? We haven't seen you since Methuselah was a pup."

"Prospected clear to the moon and back, nearly," replied David. "But now I'm through."

"You don't mean you've made your pile, do you?" asked the bartender.

"No, but I've figured out how I'm going to, and it isn't by prospecting." David tossed his sack of dust up on the bar. "I figure this'll get me started into gambling in Hangtown."

The substantial thump of the sack hitting the counter made several men turn and look. If David had turned around, he would have seen two men seated at a rough log table who continued to stare at him when the others had looked away. The heavier, coarser of the two, he wouldn't have known, but the one with the receding hairline and pockmarked face might have looked familiar. The two men exited the bar while David was still conversing with the bartender. David bought a pair of drinks for himself and the tavern man.

"You be careful, Bollin," advised the bartender as David prepared to leave. "You'd do well to wait till daybreak to travel."

"Sleeping on the trail tonight gets me that much nearer to Hangtown tomorrow. Besides, who would hold up a poor, beat-down prospector like me?" asked David, gesturing at his faded shirt, run-over boots and patched trousers. "Be seeing you."

At twilight David came to one of the numerous crossings of the stream his trail was following. A wave of tiredness compounded with the whiskey he had drunk, and David decided to make his camp for the night in a meadow just across the creek.

The water plunged through a narrow gorge at this stretch of the canyon. The bank on which he stood remained high and steep for some distance downstream, but opened out flatter on the opposite side. A fallen log rested across the gorge. The night promised to be cold, and David surveyed the log carefully. The idea of staying dry held definite appeal. He stepped up onto the log and began carefully placing one foot in front of the other as he made his way across. The tree lay not very high above the stream, and David had no fear of being injured by a fall, but the risk of losing his gold was frightening.

He watched the log for projecting stumps that might throw him off-balance. Midway across, one remaining branch poked up, offering a temporary goal and a chance to survey the remainder of the crossing.

The log rested securely on the opposite bank, caught between a large boulder and the trunk of a pine tree. An overhanging branch made the end of the log disappear in a pool of shadows, but David thought he could remember two smaller rocks by which he could climb down. He was glad to have the limb to hang on to, because he seemed a little unsteady.

Only two steps separated him from the end of the log. The branches of the pine tree stretched out toward him, beckoning him on. Another step and David reached out a hand toward the pine, expecting to grasp a branch and pull himself to the boulder.

Instead, the tree reached out toward him. A vise-like grip grasped his right wrist, and in the time it took him to shout "Hey!" it pulled him off the end of the log. He slammed headfirst into the granite rock, with an impact that caused cascades of lights to explode in front of his eyes. For a fraction of a second the exploding stars reminded him of the fireworks at the newest Kamehameha's coronation; then the lights went out.

Moffat relieved David of both pouches of gold and passed them to Barton, who stood on the ground below the rock face. Moffat rolled David over to examine the contents of the knapsack and produced the derringer. He handed it to Barton, who exclaimed, "You see! I told you this was the same busybody who interfered in Frisco. Taking his gold is like getting the rest of my own back again."

"What do you want me to do with him?" inquired Moffat.

"Bash his head and dump him in the creek," responded Barton, with no greater concern than he would show for discarding a heap of garbage. Barton leaned out from the shadows to scrutinize his derringer in the failing light.

Moffat bent over to look through a heap of stones around the base of the boulder. He spent some time selecting a rock the size and shape of a melon, and then grunted as he strained to heave it free of the thick mud.

"What's that?" Barton said sharply. The sound of shuffling footsteps came toward them on the trail.

Moffat had not heard the sound because of the rush of the creek, but he straightened up abruptly at Barton's cry.

"What's what?" he yelled back, even louder than Barton.

A voice called up the path, "Who there? What going on, please?"

A sudden oath burst from Moffat and he shouted, "Someone's coming!" The two men turned at the same instant and collided with each other. The derringer flew out of Barton's hand and he went to his knees to scrabble in the blanket of pine needles.

"Leave it! Leave it!" hissed Moffat. "Come on!" Without waiting to see if Barton was following, he plunged into the creek, not even trying to walk the log.

Barton delayed only a moment longer, then he too splashed into the stream, tightly clutching the sacks of gold. Both men were soon across and into the woods on the other side.

––––––––––

A tiny frail-looking figure in a dark blue coat cautiously advanced onto the rock. It was a Chinaman with a long silver braid. The little man bent slowly and exclaimed over David, who lay moaning softly.

The Chinaman turned to face the last waning rays of light. He tore a strip of cloth from the lining of his coat, then bandaged David's head with gentle, nimble fingers.

He kicked something in the dirt as he maneuvered around David and bent to pick it up. It was the derringer; he placed it in David's pack.

The little man's nursing had not even awakened David; he merely groaned. The Oriental bent his back until his head nearly touched the ground, then with unexpected strength lifted David onto his own shoulders. When the large young man was slung across his back like a deer carcass, the smaller, older man picked up David's pack. He began to move off down the trail, plodding slowly back the way he had come.

––––––––––

"Now you men are clear on what's to be done?" Barton addressed a scruffy group of unsuccessful prospectors who were moderately successful drinkers.

"Shore enough, Mr. Barton," responded a beady-eyed little man whose pointed nose and bristly mustache made him look remarkably rat-like. "We're just 'sposed to ease into conversations, like about how the Chinks are taking over claims us Americans oughta have."

"That's right, and any time someone volunteers that sort of sentiment, encourage them. I'll keep you in liquor and if we are as successful as I plan, there'll be better pay later."

GRABILL MISSIONARY
CHURCH LIBRARY

CHAPTER 9

David groaned and started to put a hand up to his injured forehead, but even the start of that motion sent a stab of pain through him like a bolt of lightning. *What was I drinking?* he wondered. Once when David had sneaked out at night from his father's house, he had experienced a potent native brew called *Okolehau*, which the sailors nicknamed *Oh Holy Cow*; but even it had not left him feeling this clubbed.

Clubbed, he thought suddenly. *I've been robbed!* Despite the pain he began thrashing around, trying to locate his gold sacks, but someone was holding his shoulders.

"Easy there, young fella. You've taken a nasty blow to your head. Don't try to move so fast."

"But my gold," stammered David. "Where is it, and where am I?"

"You're in a hotel in Hangtown. I should know, I run this place. As for your gold, the guy who brought you in said you'd been robbed. Said he found you up the creek a ways. He paid for the two days you've been here—"

"Two days?" interrupted David.

"Yes, and one more's paid besides. Plus," said the hotel owner, nodding toward a table beside the bed, "he left a sack of dust for you there."

117

David turned to regard a small leather pouch resting beside him. "Where is this man? I need to thank him. I mean, isn't he staying here too?"

"Course not. We don't allow—" A bell jangled in the background, causing the man to start up toward the door. "Got to go. Glad you're awake young fella." He left without completing his sentence, and the identity of David's benefactor remained a mystery.

David stretched out his hand and grasped the leather bag. He felt very weary, but he clenched his fist tightly around the gold before falling back to sleep.

The next morning David's head felt two sizes too large for his shoulders, but he was awake. The fingers of his left hand were stiff from clutching the pouch all night, and he wondered again who had befriended him without staying around to introduce himself.

The contents of the bag looked to be about two ounces of extremely fine gold dust. The sight of this small pile of shining metal reminded David of how expensive the Hangtown accommodations were and how quickly he had better make arrangements for earning more money.

But the first order of the day was breakfast. He dressed as quickly as he could, trying to keep his head motionless while he pulled on his clothes; even the slightest motion made his temples feel as if the spike that killed Sisera was being pounded home.

It was almost daybreak in Honolulu. The small guest room in the mission house, where William Bollin had spent the night, faced the huge gray outline of Kewaiahao Church and the churchyard where William's wife and children were buried.

Built entirely of hand-hewn blocks of coral, the building stood as a testimony of the spiritual changes that had come to these islands in only twenty-five years.

William sensed that he was viewing this place for the last time. He pulled on his boots and wrapped his Bible in a fresh change of clothes, then placed the bundle into his leather rucksack.

The mission family still slept upstairs. William walked softly over the wood-planked floor and stepped out onto the veranda.

With a sigh, he embraced the memories of his life one last time. At this hour, this island paradise seemed almost perfect. Life and work had grown comfortable, and William had hoped he would live out the rest of his years here.

All of that seemed of little importance now. Any price was worth it if he could only find his son alive.

William inhaled deeply. The scent of gardenias and pikake lingered in the air with a thousand other scents that drifted down from the pinnacles and up from the deep valleys of Oahu. He gathered an armful of blue flowers that tumbled over the fence and walked across the deserted yard toward the graves of his wife and children. He would say his goodbye quickly. He wanted to board the ship early, before the city awakened.

Flowers dripped in an untidy pile onto the grave of his wife.

MARTHA ELLEN BOLLIN
b. 1801
d. 1838

Ora loa ia Jesu: Endless Life by Jesus

He cleared his throat and fixed his gaze on the name carved in the black granite pillar. The stone was 5'4" tall, the same height Martha had been. It had been shipped around the Horn from her family in Boston.

"Martha," William whispered, "I would not wish you here with me this morning. I . . . I have lost him, Martha. I have won many, but lost my own son. Our son." He looked at the graves of Samuel, aged 9, and Daniel, aged 4. Tears clouded his vision for a moment. "At least you left still loving. Loving Jesus. But David loves no one, Martha. He left us without ever learning that love."

At last the sky began to lighten. The air was rose-tinged, the grass wet with dew.

He had stayed too long. Wiping his eyes, he raised his head as the morning sounds of Honolulu drifted up the road. Backing up a step, he turned to find a silent crowd gathered to wait for him beyond the stone fence of the churchyard. He had not heard them come, and even as he faced three hundred of his congregation, they did not utter a sound.

Kapono Bollin stepped carefully around the graves and nodded at Edward Hupeka, the young Hawaiian who would take his place. Edward swung back the metal gate for Kapono Bollin, and the crowd parted for him.

Murmurs of farewell rippled through the crowd, "*Aloha, Kapono Bollin . . . God go with you, Kapono Bollin!*" The small brown hands of children reached up to touch their beloved Kapono one last time. Tears traced the wrinkled faces of those who could remember the day Kapono had first brought word to them of Iesu Kristo. "*Aloha! Aloha, Kapono Bollin!*"

He bowed his head as leis of fragrant flowers were draped around his neck. "Do not forget us, Kapono Bollin! Forget not your children, Kapono!"

He had not expected this. Indeed, he had hoped to slip away without another word of farewell. But now he was glad the people had come. Looking over the sea of faces, there was not one among the crowd whom he did not know from the heart out. Births and deaths and baptisms, marriages, and twenty-five years of Sabbaths played through his mind in a moment. Moving through the crowd, he spoke their names and reached to touch outstretched fingers.

At last he stopped before the small figure of Mary.

She and her brother Edward had been abandoned at the church nineteen years before. Kapono Bollin and his wife had taken them in, cared for them, seen to their education. Now, Mary, in turn, cared for half a dozen unwanted children gathered from the villages.

Her wide-set brown eyes brimmed with tears. William took her hands in his. She spoke softly, in perfect English, "So you really are leaving, Kapono?"

"Only for a short time. Perhaps a few months."

"He has broken my heart as well, Kapono. But where shall I go? I must stay, but my heart and prayers will go with you."

William straightened to his full six feet and looked away toward the wharf and the waiting ship. He did not reply, but squeezed her hands. She was still just a child.

"Aloha, Mary."

Then he turned his back on her and raised his hands for silence as he prayed one last time with the congregation.

———

After a meal of flapjacks and bitter coffee that removed another dollar from his dwindling supply, David moved his things. He arranged to stay at a flophouse that would give him floor space for one dollar a night.

David reflected on his meager finances and shabby dress, and decided that his future as a professional gambler depended on getting some working capital—and quickly. He entered the Empire Saloon as if to do battle. He intended to start a faro game, take Lady Luck captive, and crown himself king of the gamblers.

This romantic-sounding pipedream was a sad contrast to the bleak reality of gambling at the Empire. Its wood-plank floor was covered with sawdust that was almost unrecognizable because of the liberal amounts of mud, tobacco juice, and spilled booze. The proprietor, a portly German named Finster, deliberately left the footing as unattractive as possible, to discourage miners from trying to retrieve gold dust spilled onto it. He paid a helper to shovel up and pan the debris whenever the saloon was closed. On the morning following a busy night, he might reclaim between fifty and a hundred dollars of dust.

David entered the gloomy saloon and surveyed the gaming tables. It was early in the day, and only one half-hearted game of faro was in progress. Through the thick air that smelled of stale smoke and cheap liquor, David crossed to the faro table and asked if he could join in.

The other two players and the dealer glanced at his bandaged head but nodded their acceptance, and David seated himself on an upturned half of a barrel that served as a stool. Studying the card counter, David could tell that this particular deck was about half run. He noted that no ten had yet been turned, so he placed his pouch on the pointed betting board and announced, "In for a dollar."

The next card turned was the ten of diamonds, and the dealer made a pencil mark on a scrap of paper to show one dollar in David's favor. David played steadily, never risking more than one dollar at a time and reviewing the card counter intently between plays. David was ahead by five dollars when the dealer summoned a drink for him.

David sipped the drink with evident satisfaction, studied the tally sheet, and increased his bet to two dollars. This time he backed the queen to come out next, but lost. David returned to risking only one dollar, but after winning three times in a row, he raised his stakes to five dollars.

A second drink appeared at his elbow. The five-dollar wager won, and David's spirits began to rise. *I can really do this*, he thought. *I have a sense for these cards. They speak to me.* He downed the rest of that drink and raised his bet to ten dollars.

When the ten-dollar bet was made and won, David's savings had reached almost fifty dollars and he had nearly doubled what he started gambling with. A third drink arrived and David reached out and took it without even considering why he was being kept so well-supplied. He was finding it harder to concentrate, and the drafty room began to feel oppressively warm.

The faro dealer asked for the amount of David's wager. For a moment his drink-fuddled brain refused to work, then at last he mumbled, "An ounce."

This was a sixteen-dollar bet. David indicated that he wanted his pouch of dust moved to the painted likeness of the seven card at the end of the board. David saw the dealer's eyes flicker to the back of the deck before flipping out the next card.

The oiled hides that served as window coverings at the Empire allowed in very little light. David couldn't be sure, but he thought that the dealer had made some extra motion of his ring finger before revealing the card that showed that David had lost.

David was aghast. He saw tally marks being removed from his column. His brain refused to do calculations; he couldn't determine how much of a stake he had left and wasn't able to concentrate on what card to back.

When the dealer asked for the amount of his wager, he slurred, "All of it." The dealer was pouring the contents of David's gold pouch into a hand-held pan balance before David even understood that he lost.

David's bandaged head had begun to throb. He stayed sitting dumbly, staring first at the faro table, and then down at the empty pouch that the dealer had tossed into his lap. "Will you be making another wager?" asked the dealer.

"You—you cheated me. Give me my money," David mumbled, stumbling to his feet. The other two players jumped back out of the way, knocking over their stools as they went. The dealer also rose, coming up with a gleaming knife in his right hand.

Before anything further could happen, the beefy arms of the proprietor, Finster, pinned David tightly against the white apron, which the German wore tied clear up to his chest. Finster carried him outside and deposited him in a heap in the street. "Yank man," said Finster, "I gif you some advice, no charge. Don't call no man a cheat unless you can back your play. Unt don't play no more cards mit a busted kopf." Finster dusted his hands off with authority and returned to the Empire Saloon. David staggered back to the flophouse and passed out on the floor.

———

"Gentlemen, I appeal to you on the basis of fair play and right thinking for all Americans," declared Barton to the assembled group of miners and hangers-on.

"It is our destiny to subdue this land and wrest from it the treasures for which so many now labor. Many benefits of civilization have already been bestowed on this land and much wealth produced. But I ask you, is it right that foreigners, Popish greasers, and heathen Chinese come here and take what rightly belongs to Americans? Should they be allowed to send America's treasure out of this land to benefit foreign governments?"

"Hang dem!" shouted German-born Finster.

"Let's burn 'em all out right enough," contributed Downs, whose grandparents had come to America from Yorkshire.

"No, no, gentlemen. Civilization must flourish here, and the rule of law prevail. The code of the mining community specifies how much size each claim may hold and how much work must be done to maintain it, isn't that so? We must have a meeting to amend the rules, specifying that foreigners may not hold claims. Now, who shall we have as chairman?"

———

The next morning found David more miserable than he had been since awakening to the truth of his condition on the whaler *Crystal*—worse in fact, because at least there had been food. Here he had no food, no money, and no answer in sight.

He thought briefly of begging enough food to hike back to Keo and Strawfoot, but decided against it. He reasoned that his head injury made it impossible to return to them. The truth was, he imagined himself having to explain to them what had become of his money and his ambition. He might have to admit that he had been wrong, and he couldn't bring himself to do it.

He wandered around behind the saloons and hotels, hoping to find a cook who would take pity on him, but soon discovered that he could not bring himself to beg. When he finally did get hungry enough to overcome his pride, he found that no one would give him anything. Food, like everything else, cost money to have freighted into the mines. Nothing was given away, and nothing wasted. Even the garbage was used to feed the hogs being raised for meat and lard.

After two days of starving, David found himself headed upstream, toward Strawfoot's old claim. Once there, he roused himself from his stupor enough to notice a gang of men working. They were mostly Chinese laborers, moving the stones from the wingdam that had flooded Strawfoot's diggings. As David watched, each Chinese filled a wicker basket with rocks, picked up a leather strap and, stepping inside the loop of the strap, hoisted seventy-five to a hundred pounds of rocks up onto his back. The strap rested on the worker's forehead. David thought to himself what incredibly strong necks these wiry little men must have. The largest of them could scarcely outweigh the burden being carried by more than twenty pounds.

A white man in a leather vest and a white shirt with

his sleeves rolled up was overseeing the work. He apparently spoke no Chinese, but instead transmitted his orders through a rotund Chinaman dressed in a brocade coat and silk slippers. The white foreman would give instructions to the Chinese overseer, who then relayed the order to the workers by means of much clapping, shouting, and hand-waving, and a torrent of Chinese.

David approached the line of workers. A steady stream of men in baggy trousers and matching dark blue baggy shirts toted rocks upstream to a destination David couldn't make out, returning with empty baskets for another load. With their straw hats and pigtails, the workers looked Oriental in both features and garb—except for their boots, the single concession they made to life in the Sierra gold fields.

While David looked on, the foreman consulted a pocket watch and made some comment to the overseer. With an imperious clap of his hands and a shouted command, repeated up the line of men until the message went out of earshot, all the workers shed their baskets and sat down. This was a meal break; other workers quickly began distributing paper-wrapped parcels from a hand cart. All labor ceased.

In the silence that followed, the growl of David's stomach sounded as loud in his ears as the ocean breaking on Makapuu Point. Both supervisors looked around at the sound. The Chinese man put a handkerchief to his nose as if David were as disgusting to smell as he was tattered in appearance. The white foreman rumbled, "You there—what do you want?"

David could scarcely deny that he was hungry. "Please, can you spare me some food?"

"This chow is for the coolies only. Now beat it on out of here."

"Can I have a job, then? I can haul rocks."

The Chinese supervisor laughed delicately behind his handkerchief. To laugh at a white man, even one this bedraggled, was unwise, but for a white man to ask to do coolie labor was just too droll.

"You can't be serious," said the foreman. "Why aren't you out panning for gold like everyone else? These human mules are moving rocks to make the footings for a bridge up yonder. You want to carry rocks for twelve hours a day to make a dollar?"

"And you'll feed me?" David asked.

Startled, the foreman realized that David was indeed serious. He made a quiet remark to the portly Chinaman, who shook his head and whispered something back. The white man looked David over and asked, "Isn't there anything else you can do? Don't you know anybody in town who can give you a job? What skills do you have?"

"I don't have any profession. I've been a prospector and a gambler, but right now I need food." David's stomach rumbled at that moment, as if in agreement.

"Where'd you learn words like 'profession'?" inquired the foreman.

"I did get a good education from my father. He's a preacher," David explained.

The last comment caused another flurry of whispered comments from the overseer.

The foreman listened, then said to David. "Ah Sing here says you'd be trouble. He says you'd be disruptive and a bad influence. He says he doesn't need a white man. But I am telling him now," the foreman said loudly, "that he doesn't have the final say on hiring and firing.

As the chief engineer for these Celestials, I do. And I don't want to see a white man starve while these Celestials get fed."

The foreman paused to consider, then offered, "All right, if you want food, help yourself. We're back to work in—" he stopped and considered his watch again—"ten minutes. Be ready."

He turned away from David's thanks and only grunted when David tried to tell him his name. The Chinese overseer spun around with a swirl of brocade coat, as if highly offended. David stood, uncertain who would show him where to go to get food and one of the baskets for carrying stones.

A small, thin Chinese man detached himself from the seated line of workers and approached David. With a twinkle in his eye he said, "I speak English. You come with Ling Chow. I get you food." Soon David was seated cross-legged on the ground eating rice balls mixed with pinyon nuts and a piece of broiled salmon. It was odd fare for a California Forty-Niner, but not so unfamiliar to a Hawaiian, and David devoured it eagerly.

When he was finished, David looked up from inhaling the meal to find a number of his new co-workers watching him with curiosity, and Ling Chow regarding him with a smile. He licked the last morsel of rice off of his fingers and David asked the man who had helped him, "Do many of you speak English?"

"No," the little man replied. "I speak. Not many others. All English talk-talk come to Ah Sing," he said, gesturing toward the overseer.

"Then how does it happen that you speak English?" Before the Chinaman had a chance to explain, Ah Sing clapped his hands, and another shouted order worked its way up the line. The workers replaced their baskets on their backs and began moving in their monotonous circle again. Because David had received an empty basket while Ling Chow's was filled already, the two men were soon parted and walking in opposite directions.

Once at the wingdam David soon discovered what strong necks these Chinese workers really had. When he loaded the basket to the top with stones, David could barely lift it.

Another man helped him balance the load on his back and he started walking. David found that he could not stand the pressure of the strap on his injured forehead, so he was forced to use both hands to hold the strap away from his head. In this awkward position, he was unable to use his arms for balance as did the coolies and he staggered from side to side. David tried to engage his closest co-workers in conversation, but the one ahead only turned and scowled, and the one behind grinned and giggled.

David examined the faces of the workers passing by in the opposite direction. *I hope I can remember what he looks like*, mused David. When the moment came, David didn't recognize Ling Chow again, but it didn't matter, because the friendly Chinese spoke first. He spoke as if David's question had just been asked, instead of ten minutes before. "I taught by missionaries in Sandwich Islands."

David just had time to respond, "I'm from Hawaii!" when the two men were parted again. Another ten minutes passed as David reached the building site to dump his load of stones and returned halfway back with his empty basket.

A scrap of conversation, a shouted response, and ten

minutes of plodding. This cycle continued into the dizzying afternoon. Ling Chow managed to convey to David that he had been converted to Christianity in Hawaii by Hiram Bingham, a member of the original New England Missionary Company and an old acquaintance of David's father.

It took David several baskets of rocks to decide whether or not to mention his identity. Finally the desire to establish some link with someone friendly overcame his wish to hide his background, and he mentioned his name to Ling Chow.

To his surprise, the Chinaman responded, "I know you already. I heard you tell name to boss-man. Your father Bollin a good man."

At the close of the tedious day, David received fifty cents and was dismissed until the next morning. The Chinese all bunked together in their own encampment, but David was not invited to share lodgings with them.

He went back to his flophouse and collapsed. He would have to get more money somehow, or choose between a place to sleep and eating more than once a day. At the moment he was too tired to care.

CHAPTER 10

When David awoke the next morning, his arms ached unbearably. From being held in such an awkward position the previous day, they refused to straighten out. Compounding this misery, he discovered that his flophouse bedding had been infested by "quicks"—fleas. He was bitten all over, but he couldn't make his arms reach anywhere to scratch. The decision was made for him between housing and food. Another such night, and he might also be visited by "slows"—lice. He decided to sleep out in the open, or build himself a bark shelter like the early prospectors had done. In the back of his mind lurked an awareness that winter was fast approaching, but he pushed this thought away.

David's morning improved immensely when he found that Ling Chow had brought him a tin cup of noodles, still warm in the chill air. The slight Chinaman also arranged to walk immediately ahead of David in the line, so that they could converse all day.

Ling Chow explained over his shoulder that he had wanted to return to his homeland as a missionary, but was denied that privilege. He had worked for a time with his countrymen on plantations in Hawaii, but had felt led to join the large numbers who were moving to work in California.

David did not know how to respond. How could he explain that he was running away from the same values that Ling Chow was enduring much hardship to promote?

At last he decided to say nothing about the way in which he'd left home. He referred instead to seeking his fortune in the gold field, making something of himself, and improving his prospects. He used all the phrases of a young nineteenth century gentleman. Ling Chow listened without comment, nodding as if accepting David's statements at face value. Suddenly David was struck by the irony of his attempts to sound self-assured and in control. Here he sat, eating rice among Chinese laborers, plagued by fleabites and unable even to scratch himself, with no place to sleep and no future to speak of. Who was he kidding, anyway?

That evening David found a new shelter. Ling Chow had told him about an abandoned miner's shack called a "Yankee house." It was about the size of a dog kennel and had no more comforts than one, but it had neither human nor obnoxious insect inhabitants.

David claimed squatter's rights to the place, wondering how much food he could buy for his dollar. While still considering this question, Ling Chow arrived with another pot of noodles and a small jar of some strong-smelling paste.

"What is this?" asked David, eyeing the pungent goo and wondering how he could politely refuse to eat it.

"Old Chinese remedy for bites," grinned Ling Chow. "Anyway, I am old and Chinese, and I make ointment, so is truth. Juniper berry juice and goose grease. You try."

David felt both grateful and resentful at Ling Chow's arrival. He wanted to be self-sufficient, successful, and he resented being beholden to this old Chinaman. On the other hand, he had felt so depressed and lonely that he was pleased to see someone take an interest in him. His life seemed to have taken a turn for the better since meeting Ling Chow.

The Chinaman paused at the door of the hovel, and in a kindly voice said to David, "I come this country seeking my countrymen. You come seeking something too, David Bollin. Maybe what you seek is not gold in streams like you think. Maybe you just turn around and find what you seek." No word of criticism, no demand for appreciation—just this calmly delivered cryptic advice, and he was gone.

What am I seeking? David asked himself when Ling Chow had gone. *What was it I left home to find? And what did he mean about turning around? I've come so far from home.*

The soothing ointment did its work; his spasmed muscles even began to relax, and his injured head stopped throbbing. He told God that he was not yet certain what he was seeking, but he hoped he was on the road to finding it, whatever it was. David briefly reflected that it was the first time he had prayed in years—really prayed, anyway. Then he fell asleep.

"Ching, chang Chinaman," chanted Moffat at the frightened little Oriental who was running up the alley trying to get away. "Hey, where you off to in such a hurry? Catch him, Jim, Sandy."

A pair of miners stepped out of the shadows, blocking off the line of retreat. The Chinaman glanced over his shoulders, decided the odds were better against one than two, and bolted back the way he'd come—straight into Moffat's arms.

A moment later Moffat was holding the little man off the ground by his pigtail. As the Oriental struggled and kicked, Moffat pulled a huge knife out of his belt and laid it across the Chinaman's throat. "I'd hold right still, if I was you," he hissed, "and I wouldn't make no noise, either." The smaller man complied, and Moffat lowered him until his tiptoes touched the ground, but Moffat kept a firm grasp on the queue.

"Look what I caught, boys," he remarked to the other two who had closed in around the scene. "What are you doin' outta your warren, little Chink?"

"He was prob'ly thievin'," remarked the one called Sandy.

"Up to no good, that's certain," added the other.

"Hear that, little man? I think maybe we should just go ahead and cut your throat. What do you think of that?"

The man made no response and eyed the three men in terror but made no plea.

"He don't even understand plain lingo," sneered Sandy. "He's too dumb to even remember how polite we warned him."

"He'll remember this," remarked Moffat abruptly, and he slashed the man's pigtail off short behind his head, dropping him unexpectedly to his knees. The man was up in a flash, running again down the alley, and this time they let him go.

The next day David talked cheerfully to Ling Chow while loading the first basket of rocks for the day, and smiled at his co-workers, who grinned uncertainly back at him.

"I've decided to go back upriver," he told Ling Chow. "I can own up to being wrong about leaving my partners when they needed my help. In another week I'll have enough for supplies for the trip—if," he added with a wry smile, "I keep on eating rice for a while."

"Is good you do what is right," said his Chinese friend. "God watching you all time. He help you know what to do."

"Ling, you must be right. Do you know, I never till right now thought of selling a pistol that I have. I'll never use it—why, maybe I could even leave tomorrow."

David could hardly wait for the end of the workday, and the time did seem to go by quickly. He asked Ling Chow to stop by the supply store later to tell him good-bye. After setting aside the straw basket, he hurried to his shack, retrieved the derringer, and set off for the Empire Saloon.

———

David felt ill at ease going into the saloon. He had not had a drink since the night he gambled away the last of his rescuer's gold. For a time his sobriety had been enforced by his lack of money, but now it was automatic.

He was not certain whom to approach with his request to sell the derringer, so he walked up to the only person he recognized, the German proprietor, Finster. "Mr. Finster," he began, "I'm sorry about the ruckus the last time I was in. I hope you'll accept my apology. Anyway, I'm also hoping you can help me with something else. Do you know of anyone who might be interested in purchasing this derringer?" David deposited the small pistol on the bar, and Finster leaned his bulk over to look at it.

"Maybe so," he breathed in a voice made hoarse and short by a recent consumption of a large quantity of beer and fried potatoes. "But you'll haf to vait till after our meeting. I'm busy right now."

David was disappointed. He had hoped to raise some cash on the firearm and get over to the general store across the street in time to buy supplies. David was excited at the idea of seeing Keo and Strawfoot again and wanted to make an early start of it.

Without any particular interest he asked, "What meeting is that?"

"Our committee is meeting tonight to propose a change of rules to the assembled miners. You should attend and vote. Of course there is no doubt about the outcome."

David had heard of these meetings of miners' committees, even though he had never attended one. He assumed that the rule changes concerned some issue like how many feet of creek frontage were permitted in one claim. As gold was disappearing from the streams, claims were being extended up and away from the water line. In following the twists and turns sometimes these dry land claims overlapped. Maybe this meeting was to resolve that sort of difference.

Evidently, interest ran high about whatever these rules concerned; a large number of miners arrived at the Empire Saloon for the meeting. The gambling stopped and tables were pushed closer together to allow later arrivals room to stand at the rear of the space.

Finster assumed a dignified air, puffing up his chest. He had changed his dirty apron for a clean, white one, and David thought the German moved behind the bar in a fair imitation of a heavily loaded ship under full sail.

"Mine friends—" He laid his fleshy hands palm down on the bar. "I ask you to gif attention to our chairman, Mr. Barton. I gif you Mr. Barton."

As David watched from the fringe of the crowd, the assembly parted and a tall, balding man stepped through toward the bar. He was neatly dressed and, according to the cut of his clothes, apparently well-to-do. The man shook hands with Finster across the bartop, then turned to face the group. *That's funny*, thought David, *he looks familiar to me.*

"Gentlemen, it's been my privilege to act as your chairman in this matter, and I believe we have properly discharged our duty as a committee when we issue this report for your vote. It is the committee's belief that it would be in the best interests of the Hangtown Mining District to adopt a new article, number seven in fact, to the District's bylaws."

David was bored at these proceedings. He assumed that the committee chairman was a lawyer seeking to drum up business or perhaps angling for an appointment as a justice of the peace. He decided to go on over to the store and size up the merchandise, then come back and try again to sell the pistol.

David was pushing his way through the crowd between him and the door when he heard Barton announce, "I will read you the text of the resolution, before we put it to a vote." David was carrying the small pistol by its stubby stock, the hammer upright and the barrel pointed downward.

David had reached the last ring of men between him and the door when Barton continued, " 'Be it resolved that only native Americans, which phrase shall not mean Indians, shall be permitted to hold claims or transact business for claims.' Is there any discussion?"

David stopped in his tracks, uncertain if he'd heard correctly. Only native Americans could own claims? That would mean that Ling Chow and all the Chinese could be thrown off their hard-won claims! It even meant that Keo, perhaps David himself, would be barred from owning the land they'd staked and worked and sweated over.

Barton continued smoothly, "Hearing no discussion, the chair will entertain a motion to vote—"

"Just a minute!" David cried, hopping up on a stool. "I have something to say. What gives you, or any committee, or this whole group for that matter, the right to say that people who have already been working their claims for months now can't own them?"

A voice from behind him jeered, "Ain't you the fellow that's been working with them Chinks? I know'd you was loopy when I see'd you hauling them rocks on your back like a coolie. Pay him no mind, boys, he must be half-Chinee himself."

"But the Chinese are working claims already abandoned by other miners. What harm does it do if they can make a go of some place just by working harder at it?"

Barton was dismayed to see that a low murmur from the group showed that there was some agreement with David's point. Quickly he spoke up, "Ah yes, but what about those of their fellows coming after them? If the door, which is open a crack now, is allowed to swing wide, how many millions of slant-eyed heathen will follow? I say we should slam it shut while there's still time."

A growing rumble told David that an even greater

number of miners accepted Barton's position. Shouts of "Sit down!" and "No heathen Chinks gettin' our gold!" drowned out the few who said, "Let's be reasonable, let's not be hasty."

At least I tried, David thought to himself as he stepped off the stool. After all, he could pass for American easily enough. No one need know he wasn't born in the States. He shrugged and headed for the door of the saloon.

"Look here," David heard a gruff voice shout from the saloon steps. "Them lousy Chinese even sent 'em a spy to our meeting. Look what I caught outside here, snoopin' around. What say we hand him back his pig-tail?"

Moffat was holding Ling Chow aloft by the queue in one hand while his other hand encircled the little Chinaman's throat.

At that moment something snapped in David Bollin's mind. This kindly little man who had done no one any harm was about to be injured, perhaps killed.

"No! Let him alone!" David shouted. He pushed two miners out of the way and rushed out onto the wooden sidewalk. Moffat saw him coming and threw Ling Chow to the ground. Moffat stooped to draw the knife in his boot and came up with it in his hand, intending to stab David at the end of his rush.

The light of the oil lamps gleamed on the blade at the last second before David ran on it. He threw himself to the side and brought the pistol butt down on Moffat's head, striking the bigger man on the temple.

The gun discharged with a roar that echoed under the wooden overhang. David's hand was seared from the powder blast against his palm. All movement stopped. David and Moffat stood no more than two feet apart.

Moffat was struggling with the knife. For some reason, he could not make his arm bring the point upward in the killing thrust he had planned. He watched with a stare of disbelief as his hand and arm drooped downward against his will. A dark red stain overflowed the waist of his trousers. His knees began to buckle. His mouth formed the words, "I'm shot," but no sound came. As if seeing the event in slow motion, David watched as Moffat crumpled to the ground and lay still.

David felt someone pushing him on the shoulder. He turned to see a miner trying to shove him in the direction of the street. David's ears were still ringing from the gunshot, and he saw rather than heard the man saying, "Run! Run!"

He began running up the dirt street toward his shack. The prospectors who had been in the saloon crowded the doorway so that it was several seconds before they reached the street. Once there they stood over Moffat's body. Nobody seemed anxious to face the weapon that had killed Moffat.

"Shot him clean through from stem to stern," said a grizzled miner in a slouch hat.

"Yup," agreed another. "Slug went in behind his collarbone and came out below his ribs."

"Get a doctor! Carry him in and put him on a table!" suggested one in the back of the group.

"What for?" replied his friend. "Can't you see he's stone dead? We don't need a doctor, we need an undertaker and a hunk of rope!"

CHAPTER 11

San Francisco.

William Bollin had not been prepared for the filth and squalor of the teeming city. He gazed over the jumble of tents and wooden shacks that merged at the water's edge with the hulks of once-proud ships which now served as hotels and brothels and saloons.

The discordant sounds of an off-key piano drifted over the muddy street. Smells of sewage filled the air.

Not one church steeple could be seen amid the shanty-town buildings that clung precariously to the hills. The ship's captain had been right in his description of San Francisco. Within a few square miles, the very best of every bad thing could be found. The best bad women. The best bad whiskey. The best bad gamblers. The best bad men.

Somewhere in all this, William Bollin hoped to find David. He trembled inside as he considered what his son might be involved with in such a place.

"That thar burned-out hulk is the whaleship *Crystal*," explained a saloon keeper as he pointed to the charred remains of the ship. "If yer lookin' for anyone who sailed that vessel, you'd best be lookin' up in the hills. They're all long gone. Sold their souls to the golden calf, jest like the rest of us!"

———————

His mind reeling from the sudden events, David ran up the street. Several miners called out to him, "What is it? Is someone shot?" but no one tried to stop him. David made no reply to the questions, but ran on into the night toward his shack.

An accident, he reasoned to himself. *That's all it was. I didn't mean to shoot him.* He thought about going back and giving himself up, but his legs refused to slow down.

When he reached his cabin, David sat in the darkness for a moment, not even willing to light his lantern. He had his belongings all packed and was ready to bolt out the door, when he remembered that he had not had a chance to buy supplies. He wavered between running on anyway and going back into town to explain.

As he was still trying to decide what to do, he heard a shuffling of footsteps outside the shack. He held his breath, listening to the movement outside, then a low voice called, "David, you there?"

It was Ling Chow. David burst out of the dark cabin to hug the Chinaman. "Ling Chow! Are you all right? Is that man dead? Are they coming after me? How'd you get here? Should I go back?"

Ling Chow waited for the torrent of questions to subside, then replied firmly, "Is plenty time to make decision. Is not enough time to panic."

David drew a deep breath and forced himself to slow down and listen.

Noting the way David got himself under control, Ling Chow nodded his approval. He then began to answer David's questions. Ling had left the scene of the shooting while all the miners were still gathered around Moffatt's body. Ling had heard enough to know that a lynching was being discussed, and he had brought a packet of food for David. "Is best you go away for a while," he said. "You know some place?"

David indicated that he would try to reach Strawfoot and Keo to seek their help. After that, his plan depended on the law and the mob. Ling Chow agreed. He would send word upstream in a few days to let David know how things stood.

"You good man, David Bollin," added the Chinaman in a benediction. "Maybe you save my life. God take care of you, take you home."

Stumbling up the trail in the darkness, David fell more than once over unseen rocks and roots. On one of these plunges he heard a commotion behind him, and he crawled off the trail to lie in the chaparral. A few minutes later, four men with a lantern came up the trail from town, muttering among themselves, "He wouldn't go this way."

"Naw, he'd make better time heading downstream."

"Still, he might have come this way."

All this discussion took place not ten feet from where David was lying in the dirt and sharp spines of the thicket. He lay face down, afraid that the lamp's glare on his pale face would give him away. Even when he felt some crawly thing drop onto the back of his neck, then skitter off his shoulder to the ground, he gave no sound or movement.

"Now, a fugitive wouldn't keep to the trail," one of the voices said. David's heart skipped a beat, then resumed thumping wildly when he heard, "Let's search off on the hillside over there."

After a few minutes' discussion, the group decided to go back to report their findings and obtain more lamps. David lay still a while longer, listening to their voices retreat down the trail, then cautiously raised his head to watch their lantern light dwindle to a pinpoint before disappearing.

When he rose from his hiding place, he figured that the way ahead must be clear, and he kept to the trail with as much speed as he could manage. He opened the packet of food Ling Chow had brought, devouring the rice and smoked fish as he hiked and carefully stuffing the wrapping into his pocket so as not to leave a trail. Ling Chow had also included a small leather pouch; David figured it for gold from the weight of it.

At daybreak he was on the outskirts of Washington City. Even though he knew that the trail he had followed was the only one connecting the upstream camps and Hangtown, he was afraid to be seen in town. David figured that word of the shooting would reach there later that day, and he didn't want anyone hearing his description to put the pursuers on so close a track.

As he was debating whether to stay near the town till nightfall in the hopes of obtaining more supplies or circling it in the brush and pressing on, the matter was decided for him. Up the trail from Hangtown galloped a pair of horses. From his vantage point behind a gnarled oak trunk, David couldn't see the men's faces. But from the speed of their travel, he knew they rode like men with news to deliver, and that news could only be about him.

———

As David proceeded, his travel involved tougher walking, even slower at times than the previous night.

He climbed through chaparral-covered hillsides so thick with brush that it took all his strength to push forward. At times the slopes were so steep that David had to climb them on his hands and knees. He regretted having eaten all his provisions already, for it seemed unlikely that he would get more soon.

He drank water sparingly from his bottle: his path would be over the ridges and not down near the streams. As he climbed higher, he encountered piñon pines and located some cones from which the squirrels and jays had not yet removed all the nuts. He eagerly pried them open and popped the seeds into his mouth, scouring the brush to locate more.

When night fell he rolled himself in a tarp and tucked himself as best he could into the hollow at the base of an oak tree. He tried gnawing on some fallen acorns but found them too bitter to eat, so he tossed them away in disappointment and tried to sleep.

Of course he dreamed about food. His mind painted a picture of a luau in his home village on Oahu. His nose twitched in his sleep as if smelling the fragrant steam rising from the uncovered mound of earth in which the pig had been roasting. His mouth watered as his subconscious remembered baked yams and fresh mangoes.

The chill air made him hunch more closely into his bedroll. The scene in his dream mind shifted, transporting him to the Nuuanu Pali, with its sheer six hundred foot drop. He saw himself in the role of a Hawaiian warrior opposing King Kamehameha the First, being driven back toward the precipice. The sides of the Pali were closing in and there was no place to scale them or to circle around the oncoming forces. At the last moment, David's dream figure hurled a spear at his opponent, then leaped, screaming, over the cliff. He woke with a sudden start, his body rolling abruptly against a tree root and his stomach still refusing to give up the notion that he was falling through air.

A rim of frost covered the ground, and the dull gray sky held no promise of warmth for the day. David was debating whether to stay in his canvas cocoon until the sun was full up, or unroll it and build a fire. A movement in the brush froze him in place, half in and half out of the tarp.

It was not the noise of a man walking; indeed, no man could arrive at David's sleeping place without a lot of crashing of brush and snapping of twigs. The sound that accompanied the motion sensed by David was a padding sound, a weight pressed carefully against the earth in an unhurried rhythm that seemed to flow up the hill toward him.

An instant later a mountain lion stepped through the chaparral into David's view. Man and lion regarded each other from a distance of a dozen feet.

The lion was sleek and well fed, with powerful muscles that rippled beneath its tawny hide. Its yellow eyes locked on to David's in an embrace of mutual fascination. The man had to tear his eyes away from the cat's before he noticed the limp form of a rabbit hanging from the lion's jaws.

David bolted upright, struggling with his canvas covering and thrashing around to free himself. The cougar, startled by the sudden movement, lashed its tail and leaped across the clearing into the brush. With a parting snarl, it dropped the rabbit before disappearing up the slope.

David blinked at the spot where the lion had been a

moment before. For an instant he wondered if anything could actually disappear from view so quickly. Perhaps the lion had been another part of his dream, just before he was fully awake.

Then he saw the rabbit, lying on the hillside just beyond the circle of leaves shed by the oak tree. He struggled again to free himself and this time succeeded.

A few minutes later, the rabbit, minus its fur and entrails, was impaled on a forked branch and roasting over a small fire. He tore off a half-cooked hind limb and began devouring it, while continuing to roast the remainder.

David was pleased at the lucky accident that had brought the lion up the hill by this path at this time. If he had still been sleeping, the lion would have passed unseen. A few moments later, he would have been up, making enough noise for the lion to have heard and chosen a different path. The odd coincidence that the predator had recently killed but not yet devoured its prey also entered David's mind.

Finally Ling Chow's promise that God was interested in David's well-being broke into his conscious thoughts. He wasn't sure what it meant, but the idea that God was watching him made David uncomfortable. Somehow David's picture of God and the memory of his pastor father were mixed up together, and he felt a surge of remorse.

Hangtown buzzed with a discussion of Moffat's death for about a week. Riders dispatched to the neighboring mining communities carried David's description and an account of the crime, but the mob's interest in tracking him dissipated after the first night.

The shooting had interrupted the vote on the issue of the mining rights of foreigners. Try as he might, Barton could not get the discussion started again. He tried to press the notion that the shooting had been a deliberate attack in which the Chinese were conspirators, but nobody bought it.

What really caused the interest of the town to shift away from Barton's proposal was not any change in attitude toward foreigners, but the arrival of a new immigrant—a woman from Missouri, and the first woman many a miner had seen in almost a year.

She had been coming overland to California with her husband and their small child, a girl, when the man had been taken ill with cholera and died. Now she and her daughter had arrived at the destination for which they had planned, but without the husband and father to build their cabin and prospect for gold.

She sat in the back of her wagon, numbly pondering their future, when a grizzled miner approached. His beard was bushy and black as coal and his wiry hair was smashed flat by the slouch hat he wore, only to escape around his neck and shoulders like an immense scrub brush. He wore two revolvers in his belt, the handles reversed for a cross-draw. The hilt of a bowie knife protruded from his boot top, and his fierce eyes gleamed out from the thicket of hair, adding to his savage appearance.

He approached the rear of the wagon and stood glaring at the canvas flap through which the woman was watching his arrival with some misgivings. She was uncertain whether a call for help would scare this menacing figure away or rouse him to violence.

Presently he swept off the slouch hat, and in a loud

voice remarked, "Ma'am, if you're at home, may I speak with you?"

The woman made no reply, but timidly drew aside the canvas. The miner stepped up to peer into her face. He seemed to be in a trance as he drew several deep breaths without speaking. At last he said, "I have a family back in the States. I came to California so as to make enough money to buy land to go to farming. I've been cold, wet, hungry, scared, disappointed and dejected. I'd almost forgot what I was working for, till I saw you and . . . is that a child there?"

The woman nodded that it was indeed. Her daughter lay asleep with her head resting against her mother's knee. The fierce-looking prospector stepped up closer to the wagon, stretched out his hand, then stopped, lifting his eyes to meet the mother's. She smiled and nodded briefly. The miner continued to reach out his hand until just the tips of his rough, scarred fingers brushed the little girl's hair.

His hand began to tremble and he drew back, fearful that his nervous shaking might awaken the child. He replaced his slouch hat, and with one hand loosened the rawhide ties that connected a small leather bag to his belt. The miner laid the pouch on the tailgate of the wagon and stepped back, gruffly murmuring "much obliged," as he turned to leave. One gnarled and hairy fist gouged at his eyes as he sought to clear away the tears coursing down his cheeks. Ten yards away he stopped and looked back toward the wagon. "Mrs.—?"

"Parker," the woman replied, looking straight into the miner's eyes. "Mrs. Parker."

"Thank you, Miz Parker," he finished. "Thank you for coming."

The woman examined the pouch curiously, pouring out a small pile of gold into her palm. Breathing a prayer of thanks, she carefully returned the precious dust to its bag, then raised her eyes to look across the clearing. There, in a silent, respectful line, stood a hundred miners, waiting for a glimpse of her and the child. At each belt was tied a small leather bag.

Barton watched this scene with an amused and cynical eye. He saw no way in which he could profit from the miners' sentimentality. In fact, he felt vaguely threatened by the notion that civilization and a gentler spirit might be arriving in the hills.

Above everything else, Barton knew that to recapture the attention of the town and rekindle interest in the scheme to drive out the foreign miners, he would have to show his leadership. He would have to take public, personal charge of bringing Bollin in to face trial and hanging. It might be even better if Bollin put up a fight and was killed resisting.

The day Pastor William Bollin arrived in Hangtown, rain was falling in sheets. The runoff coursed down the main street in such a torrent that one could almost believe that the town was built with a creek in its middle. Pastor Bollin lifted his face to the cold, gray skies and felt very far from Hawaii, indeed.

He had walked all the way from San Francisco. His congregation had given him a generous gift, but between the cost of passage to California, at Gold Rush prices, and his new outfit of gear suitable for a Sierra winter, there wasn't much left.

From the brow of the hill that hung over the town,

Pastor Bollin got occasional glimpses as the wind swirled the curtain of rain aside. It was not a very inviting scene. Behind what must have been the livery stable, a few mules stood in companionable misery with their heads drooping and rain dripping from their soaked hides. An occasional human figure could be seen, but only making a dash from one doorway to another.

Pastor Bollin had not fixed his destination as Hangtown because of any definite news of David. Instead, he had decided to start his search in this soggy outpost because its name had been mentioned more often than any other in overheard conversations in San Francisco. Now that he had arrived, he was not at all sure where to begin inquiring.

Through a break in the storm, Pastor Bollin could make out one sign on top of a building at the far end of town. *Empire*, it said. The preacher fixed his bearings on this target and began descending the muddy slope. The main street was a more direct route, but travel there seemed to require hipboots at least, if not a rowboat. The side streets were a little less waterlogged, but they zigzagged so much that Pastor Bollin lost his way and spent thirty minutes covering the last half mile.

Once under the Empire's wooden awning, Bollin took off his heavy coat and shook it out, then removed his felt hat and wrung what seemed like a pint of water out of it. He ran his hands through his graying hair to restore it to some sort of order before stepping inside.

The Empire was clearly a saloon and a gambling parlor, full of disreputable-looking characters. Pastor Bollin shuddered at the thought that he felt led to such a place to ask about David's whereabouts. The smoky room was only slightly less muddy than the street outside. Behind the counter, a large man with a dingy white apron tied high up on his chest wiped up spilled whiskey with a bar towel. As the reverend watched, the man took the same rag and rubbed it lazily over some glasses, which he then placed upside-down on the shelf behind the bar.

"What you haf?" asked the bartender in a guttural accent. "Whiskey?"

"No, thank you," replied the preacher. "I'm really in search of information."

"Dis iss not a libarary," replied Finster curtly. "Conversation iss only free for customers."

"All right then, what have you got to eat?"

"Beans iss what vee got. A dollar a bowl. You vant some?"

"Sure," agreed William Bollin, laying a coin on the bar.

"What iss that? I never see a dollar or a peso like that before."

"It's a Hawaiian coin. In San Francisco they took it as fair exchange for a dollar."

The big German eyed the coin suspiciously. "Unt where did you come by such a piece?" he asked.

"I'm from Hawaii," the preacher replied. "Actually, I'm not a miner. I'm here looking for my son."

"You don't look like no Kanaka fella," said the bartender, shaking his head in disbelief.

"No," responded Pastor Bollin with a chuckle, "but I've been there long enough to think like one. I'm a missionary, you see, a preacher. As I say, I'm here—"

Finster interrupted with an explosive guffaw, and then in a loud voice that rolled over the murmured conversations around the gaming tables, called out, "Guess vot ve got here, boys! A preacher-man! What brand of preacher iss you? Ve had a Methodist kind here but ve gave him a ride out of town, didn't ve, boys?"

"Look," said William Bollin with dignity, "I didn't come in here looking to preach at you. My name is Pastor William Bollin, and I'm looking for infor—"

From a large table in the center of the room rose a well-dressed man with a receding hairline and an air of self-importance. He strode up to the preacher and stopped the noise of the room by holding up his hand in an order for silence. "What did you say your name was?" he demanded.

"My name is William Bollin, and I'm looking for my son, David. Do you know his whereabouts?"

"Not yet, but I will soon. Your son is a wanted man, preacher, but I aim to bring him to justice."

"Thank the Lord he's alive! But wanted for what? What's he done?"

"Done? Just cold-blooded murder, that's all. He got drunk and killed a business associate of mine who was just enforcing some of the rules we have around this town to keep out riffraff and foreigners."

"I don't believe it," maintained Pastor Bollin stoutly. "David may be in trouble, but I want to hear his side before I'll believe that he's a killer."

"You'll get to hear his side all right—right after my men bring him in, and right before we hang him."

"You won't hang him until we've heard from other witnesses," said the preacher grimly. "I'll make it my job to dig out the whole story."

"I knew you'd be a troublemaker, soon as I heard you were a preacher," said Barton, appealing to the gamblers with outstretched arms. "Isn't that right, boys?"

Barton's extended left hand curled into a fist, and he

swung it around in a short arc that connected with the preacher's nose, knocking him back against the bar. "Jim, Sandy, throw this foreign gospel sharp out into the street."

Two men rose from a nearby table to comply. They dragged William Bollin through the muck and trash of the saloon floor, his nose gushing blood. At the doorway they paused only long enough to swing him back and forth twice before heaving him into the muddy street.

Barton stood in the doorway rubbing his bruised knuckles. "I'll give you some advice, preacher. We don't want your kind in this town. Being kin to a murderer doesn't endear you to our hearts, either. If I was you, I'd head straight back to wherever I came from." With that, Barton turned on his heel and went back inside the Empire Saloon.

Once back inside, he called Sandy and Jim and two others over to him. "Rain or no rain, you get out there and get on Bollin's trail now. I want him found before anyone else comes around talking about witnesses and justice, understand?"

Pastor Bollin lay in the muddy street, momentarily stunned. He shook his head to clear it, and raised his chin to let the rainwater wash away the blood from his face and restore him to clear thinking. He was puzzled by the fact that he did not feel more distressed about the news of the murder accusation. Then it came to him with a thudding awareness more substantial than Barton's fist: David was alive!

Kapono Bollin lifted his hands toward the stormy sky. "Thank you, Lord," he whispered as tears of joy began to choke back his words. "My son, who was dead, is alive! Dear God, David is *alive*!"

After months of anguish and grief, Kapono Bollin had proof at last that David still lived—at least as recently as the shooting. But how to find him? And how to protect him from the lynch law in this place?

A pair of muddy boots walked into Pastor Bollin's view, and a hand reached down to help him to his feet. The preacher looked up into the ruddy face of a man of medium height who wore his hair neatly trimmed. "Friend," the man said, "I don't know who you are, but you look too respectable to have been thrown out of the Empire for not paying your tab, so you must have found some other way to antagonize them. If a man is known best by his enemies, you're the right sort for me. Come along."

"Where are you taking me?" asked the pastor with understandable concern, given his Hangtown welcome.

"There are some upstanding folks in this town. Most of them gather at Widow Parker's eating place. My name is Morris," added the man with a firm handshake and a pleasant smile. "We'll see about getting you a hot meal and some dry clothes, and you can tell me how you came to be on the cross-grain side of Barton."

CHAPTER 12

Olivia Parker did not fit Pastor Bollin's image of the kind of woman who would run a restaurant in a place like Hangtown. Tall and slim, with a ready smile and a homespun kind of attractiveness, Mrs. Parker brought a welcome ray of grace and gentility to a rough and hostile environment.

"I guess she did most of her grieving on the trail after her husband's death," Morris had told Bollin as he filled the pastor in on the woman's history. "By the time she got here, she was pretty determined to pick up the pieces and get on with life—maybe as much for her daughter's sake as for her own."

Morris stood aside and held open the door of a low, pole-supported building of rough-sawn timber. It had been a storage shed before Mrs. Parker bought it, he said. In the short time since receiving the donations from the miners, she had purchased the building, had some windows cut in the sides, and put down planks to cover the bare earthen floor. All the labor involved crowded out her sorrow and grief with practical concerns.

Mud still squished up between the planks, but the inside was clean, cheerfully lighted by oil lamps. Widow Parker served no liquor and allowed none to be consumed on the premises, but the miners did not seem to mind. Her wholesome cooking and kindly disposition attracted them.

She welcomed the man named Morris as a favored customer, and clucked with sympathy over the injury to Pastor Bollin's nose. She bustled around, directing the preacher to a side room in which to get out of his soggy gear. She brought him a set of dry clothes—a barter struck a week before in exchange for a meal—and fixed a chair for him close to the fire.

When Bollin was settled comfortably, Mrs. Parker brought him a steaming bowl of soup. "Oxtail soup," she announced. "Very nourishing. Now, no questions until he's drunk every last drop," she instructed Morris firmly.

When he had consumed the pleasantly fragrant broth, Pastor Bollin thanked his hostess, and pronounced himself ready to tell his story. Mrs. Parker, Morris, and a group of others gathered around. Bollin explained who he was and the events that had led up to his untimely departure from the Empire Saloon. At the mention of the pastor's name and his search for his son, a bearded man with a shock of black hair looked up abruptly, glanced over his shoulder, and left the restaurant.

"So you see," Pastor Bollin was concluding just as the bearded man returned, "now I know that I haven't come all this way for nothing; David really is alive. God has brought me directly to this place to find him and help him."

"And we will help you, Kapono Bollin," announced a voice from the doorway. The burly, white-haired form of Keo Kekua entered Mrs. Parker's, accompanied by Strawfoot, who had gone to fetch him.

"Keo! Keo Kekua!" Pastor Bollin stammered.

"What—what are *you* doing here?" The shock of seeing a familiar face was almost too much for Bollin, and he started to sink back down in his chair.

Keo, however, never gave him the chance to sit. He grabbed the pastor and lifted him bodily off the ground in an enthusiastic hug. Tears filled the big Hawaiian's eyes as he laughed, "Kapono! Kapono Bollin!"

"Put him down, Keo," Strawfoot insisted. When Bollin was safely deposited in his seat, Strawfoot recounted the events leading up to David's part in Moffat's death.

"We were all partners after we met up in San Francisco," Strawfoot finished, indicating Keo with a nod of his head. "David—uh, left the partnership, and we kinda lost track of him. When we got word of the trouble he was in, we came down to help."

"Kawika good man," Keo put in. "He in trouble, but he not murder nobody."

"I'm just glad he's alive," Kapono Bollin said softly. "Whatever trouble he's in, we'll find him—before that man Barton does."

"Excuse me for butting into this reunion," interrupted Morris, "but I want to help also. A friend of mine was killed in San Francisco, shortly after catching Barton cheating at cards. David is known to have been a witness. I have obtained a writ requiring Barton to return to Frisco for questioning, but here I find him practically running the town. In fact, I felt it necessary to send the Chinese who witnessed Moffat's death away to Sacramento for safety."

"That's where I come in," added Mrs. Parker. "I was received here with such kindness that I cannot believe that the majority of miners want anything to do with Barton's brand of evil and lawlessness. And—" She stopped to retrieve a folded poster from a pocket of her apron. "Look at this."

The poster displayed a likeness of Barton and the words *WANTED FOR FRAUD*. Underneath, the small print added that Barton was known to be a cheat at cards, and was often in the company of a suspected murderer named Moffat. "I picked this up accidentally with some dress patterns at a dry goods counter in St. Joe," explained the widow. "It wasn't until I was unpacking my things here the other day that it came to light. Don't you see the hand of God in this, Reverend? This paper came all the way across the plains with me, and I didn't know anything about it until it was needed."

All the men were speechless for a minute, then Pastor Bollin asked, "Since this Barton is clearly not the man to be running a town, how is it that he remains in charge?"

"He's surrounded himself with a group of strongarm types," Morris answered. "They have the support of a group of malcontents and complainers looking for someone to blame for their own failures. The crowd would desert him quick enough if he didn't have his crew of self-appointed shoulder-strikers pretending to be policemen."

"Is there enough sentiment among the decent folks to arrest Barton and hold him on the various charges if his bullies weren't around?" asked Pastor Bollin.

"There certainly is," agreed Morris. Mrs. Parker nodded vigorously.

"Well then, friends, we must pray that God sees fit to separate Barton from his henchmen, and protect my son David at the same time."

David traveled as far as he could toward Strawfoot's claim, but he struggled through thick brush and up rocky slopes. The trail itself went through such rocky gorges and along such treacherous dropoffs that it was impossible to try to travel it at night. That left David moving in daylight to avoid breaking his neck, but increased the likelihood of his being captured and having his neck stretched. He continued trudging over steep ridges and following rocky ravines, only to find that he had to climb out of them straight up granite walls. His hands were torn and bloody, and the sense of well-being he'd had after eating the rabbit had long since disappeared.

The wind that began to whistle down from the Sierra summits had a bite to it, threatening that the night would be bitterly cold. David recognized that he'd better use the daylight that remained to locate a sheltered place to spend the night. Up ahead he spotted another narrow ravine like the ones he had been climbing into and out of all day; this one seemed to beckon with the promise of a safe haven from the wind and a place secluded enough to build an unnoticed fire.

From the lip of the canyon, David saw that it was a steep climb down, not appearing to have running water at the bottom. Both factors made it unlikely that it was occupied by humans, or that his pursuers would seek him there. David examined his swollen and aching fingers, then flexed his hands and felt how stiff they were getting. He could not delay any longer, or the descent would be impossible.

The first part of the climb he made from handhold

to handhold, bracing himself on the trunk of a cedar tree while looking for the next rocky ledge. Then his feet slipped on a thin patch of gravel that concealed a smooth rock face, and he began to slide downward. David threw himself backward against the cliff, flat on his back, with a jolt that jarred his head. Momentarily stunned, he flung his arms out in a desperate attempt to stop the motion toward an even steeper part of the cliff that dropped off into space.

His arms found nothing to grasp, and his boots skittered over the slide-rock as if they had a life of their own and were determined to throw him off the cliff. He tried to find something to catch a heel on, but encountered nothing. *No one will ever find my body*, he thought briefly as his legs shot out into the air over the dropoff.

All at once his movement stopped. With a twang like a bowstring, his body hit the end of its slide, and an unseen hand seemed to yank him back from the edge. David hung there, suspended over a fall whose height he could not even guess, much less see. His backpack had caught on some tiny unevenness in the rock, but how securely he could not tell.

David lay completely still, pressing himself tightly against the rock. He was afraid to raise his head to look around and afraid to move his arms to hunt for a handhold, fearing that even the slightest movement would dislodge whatever held him and throw him over the edge. Even the prayer he breathed was delivered cautiously, as if too vigorous an exhaled breath would become his last. He tried to think what to do by picturing himself as an onlooker trying to coach someone out of this predicament.

A voice in his head told him to bend his knees. They

had been locked, holding his lower legs out straight over the void. Gently and carefully, he allowed them to fold downward. His heels bumped into the rock. There was a ledge, just above where his feet were hanging. Ever so slowly he raised one boot until the heel bumped in to rest on a narrow seam of rock. Carefully he repeated the process with the other foot so that both feet were resting on a two-inch lip of stone.

David pushed downward on first one foot and then the other, testing to see if the ledge would bear his weight. Even after he felt that it was secure, he hesitated. Finally, he raised his body until he was sitting on the edge of the cliff with his boot heels supported by the tiny rim of rock.

Peering over the edge, David could see that it was a forty-foot drop to the canyon floor. He might have survived the fall, only to die of starvation after breaking every bone in his body. Despite the chill in the air, sweat trickled off his forehead into his eyebrows.

The ledge angled downward into the gloomy shadows that already filled the ravine, but David could follow its path far enough to know that it led to safety. Just a few feet to the left of his heels the rocky step widened out into a narrow path. Scooting his body gently along the edge, David reached the point where his heels would no longer touch. Holding his breath again, he stood upright. The ledge held his weight, and the increased width gave him room enough to spin his body around and press his stomach against the rockface. Once this was accomplished and he was breathing again, he began to creep down the angled verge of the cliff.

David was trusting his feet to feel their way along. His face rubbed against the stone and his eyes darted from one tiny handhold to the next so that he would have a secure grasp if the ledge gave way. His face pressed into the rock and the shadows increasing, he didn't see the rope hanging down the rocky slope until his nose ran into it. Even then it took him a moment to grasp the significance: if there was a rope hanging down this canyon, then humans had been there before. They might, in fact, still be there.

David leaned backward, out from the wall, and turned his head slowly to look around. The path on which he stood led all the way down to the ground, but his eyes had to adjust to the darkness before he could make out the cabin. It was actually just the front of a cabin, a wall of hewn logs set into a recess in the rock with a door of rudely split planks in the middle.

David hung there, trying to decide what his next move should be. Clearly, he could not go back up the way he had descended. The cabin's builder had hung the rope to assist his entrance and exit, but David's battered hands and shaking legs would not support such a climb. He listened for the sounds of human activity, but didn't hear, see, or smell anything that betrayed the presence of another.

The final few feet to the canyon's bottom proved an easy crossing, and in a moment David stood outside the door. "Hello?" he called, hoping anxiously that he would get no answer, and not at all sure what he would do if one came. Silence continued in the dark ravine, and David pushed open the wooden door. By the waning light he could make out a candle stub on a tin holder in the middle of a rough table. Alongside the candle, in readiness for the owner's return, lay a handful of matches. David struck one of these on the tabletop, and lit the candle, then began to peer around the room.

Only the front wall of the structure was made of wood. The rest of the cabin was a natural alcove of the rock, roughly boxlike in shape with the stone ceiling about eight feet high at the front, but sloping downward toward the rear. A heap of rocks formed a partial wall joining floor and ceiling, forming a ledge along which the owner's belongings were laid.

A duffel bag such as a common seaman used was lying there, but of much greater interest to David was a partially full sack of flour. There seemed to be no other food around, but even this looked enticing. A charred ring of stones and a gap in the wooden wall directly above it indicated the builder's cooking facilities.

David soon located a frying pan, but hadn't yet found any water. Poking around the rear wall again, he discovered another reason for the built-up ledge of stone: a seep of moisture oozed out of the rock face, and a catch basin had been made to hold a small pool of the cold, clear water. The basin was full, and the surplus ran downward again through cracks in the rocky floor; no one had been at home here for some time.

David went out to gather some small dead branches and brush and soon had a cheerful fire blazing. He mixed flour and water and cooked a flapjack the size of the skillet. It was burned in places and raw in others, but he ate it happily before falling asleep beside the fire.

———

"Hey, where is everybody? Pastor Bollin, Mrs. Parker, Morris, hang it all, are you all deaf? Wake up!" The excited voice of Strawfoot broke the stillness of the dawn at Mrs. Parker's restaurant, and he pounded on the door for good measure.

From behind the hanging blanket that partitioned off Mrs. Parker's sleeping area, the sleepy voice of a child could be heard asking, "What is it, Mommy?"

"Just a minute, Sugar, I'll go see." Mrs. Parker belted a dressing gown around herself, and went to the door, stepping around the form of Pastor Bollin, who was sleeping by the fire, and past the bench that held the recumbent outline of Morris.

Opening the entrance a crack, she peered out. "Yes, Mr. Strawfoot, what is it? And what time is it? Everyone is still sleeping."

Strawfoot looked surprised. "Why, I beg your pardon, Ma' am, but it's well past five. I just figgered everybody would be up and anxious to hear the news."

"We're certainly up now, Mr. Strawfoot," the widow agreed, gesturing over her shoulder at the stirring men. "What is this news?"

"After last night's discussion, me and Keo decided we oughta keep an eye on Barton and his gang. Well, not thirty minutes ago, they rode out."

"Who rode out?" asked Morris, now wide awake. "How many of his men are gone?"

"Ain't that just what I've been tryin' to tell you? All of 'em! That sandy-haired feller, the one they call Jim— the whole lot of them."

"What? You mean to say Barton is in town without any of his close associates?"

"That's exactly what I do say," replied the prospector.

"Did you hear that, Pastor?" asked Mrs. Parker. "Your prayer has been answered. We can get a group of concerned citizens together and arrest Barton today. We'll have this town cleaned up in a week."

"What you say is sure enough true, ma'am," continued Strawfoot, "but we'd best keep on a'prayin' for David."

"Why yes, but—"

"Don't you see, ma'am? The reason they skedaddled in such a hurry is to hunt down David. I heard Barton as they was leavin'. 'Bring him back,' he said. 'Alive if you can, but dead is all right with me!' "

———

The next day dawned gray and cloudy, and a light rain started falling. Through gaps in the ridgelines around, David looked up the mountains toward the higher country and the passes he would have to cross to reach Keo and Strawfoot. As he watched, they became obscured in a swirling haze that at first dulled and then veiled the stretches of hillside forest. David had never encountered it before, but he had heard enough about snow to recognize the first storm of winter. If it continued falling and the weather stayed cold, he would have to give up his idea of rejoining his two companions.

For the time being he was content to remain where he was. He felt secure, convinced that not only was the cabin's builder absent, but he was never going to return. He gave some thought to the lack of food, but decided that he could trap rabbits or quail, given the time to remain in one location safely. In any case, he was optimistic about his immediate future for the first time since the shooting.

For breakfast he cooked another flapjack, then used more flour and water to form a crude lump of dough which he nestled among the heated stones of the firepit to bake for later. This accomplished, his curiosity finally caused him to dump out the contents of the seabag onto the stone counter.

The duffel bag seemed like a treasure trove. Out of it tumbled a heavy sweater, an oilcloth jacket and matching trousers, long underwear, heavy socks, a waterproof hat and a pouch containing gunpowder, percussion caps and shot. David was still carrying the derringer around in his backpack, though he had never had but the one charge for it.

Eagerly David discarded his worn-out clothing and after bathing with handfuls of water from the small pool, dressed himself in his newfound gear. The pants were a little short, but in general the fit was not unmanageable.

David reloaded the pistol and went out to explore the ravine. Just as he had seen from above, the canyon's walls were sheer everywhere except for the place he had descended. The canyon floor was only wide for a couple of hundred yards, then it pinched off again at both ends, becoming almost too narrow to pass through. In addition, the upper end was blocked by a rockslide, so only the downslope direction offered any possible exit, and it seemed to plunge into an even more precipitous stretch of ravine.

Exploring done, David returned to the cabin. He removed the baked crust from the stones and munched on it thoughtfully. The prospects of trapping anything on the canyon floor did not seem so good after all, but in another day or so his hands would be recovered enough to be able to make the climb out using the rope. The surrounding hillsides would certainly provide some game, especially now that he had a usable firearm.

David imagined himself hunting with the derringer,

drawing a bead on a squirrel and carrying it home to cook. He thought of himself as Robinson Crusoe, making a home in the little canyon as if it were a deserted island.

Remembering how his father had read Defoe's book to him when he was ten or eleven years old made him miss his home in Hawaii. He thought of his father with real longing, and his storybook sensation dissipated. The reality of his situation hit home: he was alone in a wilderness with winter coming on, and he was being hunted outside this narrow little world as a murderer.

I'll go home, he thought. *I don't know why I didn't think of it before. If I can get back to Frisco without getting caught, I can work my way home on a sailing ship. I'll say to my father that I'm sorr—*

His thoughts were violently interrupted as the door to the cabin burst open. For an instant David thought that a freak gust of wind had caused it: then he saw the form of a man standing in the gray rain. "What are you doing in my place with my belongings?" demanded a strangely chanting voice. When David made no reply, the man advanced into the room and threw off the sodden hat that had hidden his features.

A thrill of fear burst up David's spine and raised the hair on the back of his neck. It was Greaves! David had last seen the captain of the *Crystal* being dumped into San Francisco Bay by Keo, right after his pistol shot had creased David's cheek. Instinctively, David's hand went up to the location of the old wound, now faded to a thin scar. He pulled his hand back down, but not before Greaves had seen the gesture.

Greaves took another step into the shelter. He leaned forward to peer at David. His eyes widened and his face became a mask of hatred. "It's you!" he panted. "How

I've thought about this day! You, who burned my ship, stole my life, ruined me! Now I find you here, stealing from me again!"

"Captain, I . . . the fire . . . I didn't . . ."

Greaves gave him no opportunity to explain about the ship. "I'll strangle you with my bare hands!" Greaves lunged forward across the room, seeking David's throat.

David jumped aside, pulling the derringer from his belt as he did so. He leveled it at the sea captain and warned him to stay back. "You lily-livered swine!" Greaves yelled. "You haven't got the courage to pull the trigger. You only work by stealth. Fire and flame. Blazing destruction! The *Crystal*, my *Crystal*!" Specks of foam began to appear at the corners of Greaves' mouth. His eyes unfocused, and a second later he charged David again.

Greaves had been partly right. David couldn't say what had stopped him from pulling the trigger, but he let Greaves crash past him again. He had already planned his next move: he made a grab for the pouch of shot and powder, and ran out the door into the rain.

Down the canyon he went, leaping over boulders and racing toward the narrow exit from the ravine. He pulled away from Greaves, whom he could hear pounding after him, and went sliding over a huge rock. He landed heavily, but got up and continued running. The crazed captain apparently stopped following at the rock, but his voice echoed after David down the twisting defile, "I'm on to you now! I'm on your trail again! I'll never rest until you're dead! Dead, do you hear me? Dead!"

The last word echoed and bounced off the rocky walls of the canyon, and seemed to chase David for a long time before finally dying away.

CHAPTER 13

David leaned against a rock and breathed heavily, his sides aching and his chest on fire. He tried to take stock of his situation while watching up the canyon to see if Greaves was following. He held his breath to listen for the sounds of pursuit; otherwise his own rasping was all he could hear.

He recovered enough to move on again, but more slowly, trying to think as he went. He regretted the loss of his backpack and bedroll, but he had gained the warmer clothing and waterproof covering. In addition, he now had a supply of ammunition and still possessed Ling Chow's pouch of gold.

Instinctively, he thanked God for the new clothing and for delivering him from Greaves without the necessity of killing the captain, astonished at how radically his attitudes had changed. And now that he had decided to go home, he was also grateful for his new sense of direction.

David chuckled hoarsely to himself that he could find things to be appreciative for his present situation. Ling Chow would approve; Keo would be amazed.

Eventually the canyon he was descending became too dangerous for him to follow, and he looked for a way to climb out. But the rain had made the rocks slick, so he located a flattened bench of stone on which to rest. Against the wall of the arroyo, a slight overhang offered some protection from the downpour, and into this crevice he pressed himself.

He had intended only to rest a short while before continuing, but the combination of fear, excitement and relief overcame him. When he awoke it was pitch black, and even though the rain had stopped, David decided against continuing upward before dawn.

When morning came again to the Sierra Nevadas, David woke up feeling as if something were wrong with his ears. It was too quiet, unnaturally still. When he opened his eyes, he saw why: the snow which had been falling at the higher elevations the previous day had moved lower. Everything around him was covered with a thin white blanket that muffled noises as if nothing were stirring at all, as if the whole world, except David, still lay asleep.

He shook off the little bit of snow that had landed on his back and legs and stood up. The air was crisp, but not too frosty, and the sun rising over the line of peaks promised some warmth later in the day.

David had never seen snow before, and he scooped up a handful. He marveled at its coldness and the way it could be pressed together. He tossed his first snowball into the canyon below and made another.

David amused himself by making the snowballs smash on a large rock at the base of the canyon wall. He tried an experimental mouthful of the glittering substance and wished that he could have seen it falling.

The fully risen sun now burst into his sight, its rays illuminating the snow-covered hills. The glare lit up the stretch of canyon before him. By the sharp contrast between dark rock walls and brilliant snow, David could see a long way back up the ravine. Very far up, but coming toward him, he could make out a solitary figure. It had to be Greaves.

David threw his last snowball away and turned to climb up the rock face. Once out of the canyon he began to run down the snowy slope on the other side, occasionally sliding and having to catch on to the branches of oak trees to keep from falling. Each time he grabbed a tree branch, a shower of snow fell on his head, and his progress downhill looked like a series of crystalline explosions. Rolling hills lay before him, their tops covered with snow, as far as he could see.

After crossing several of these hills, David saw smoke rising from a hollow ahead of him. Smoke meant another mining camp, another danger to be avoided. But smoke also meant food and he'd eaten nothing since the crust of burnt dough a whole day before. He tried to put that thought out of his mind and moved to circle the rim of hills that bordered the little community.

When he was directly above the camp on the slope, a breeze caused the smoke to drift toward him. Instantly his nose reported that the smoke was not just campfires, but a hundred miners cooking their bacon and boiling their breakfast coffee.

It's early yet, David's mind suggested. *I could go in and grab supplies and get out while everybody is rustling their grub. Nobody will give me a thought.* David's stomach rumbled its agreement, and suddenly it was easy to ignore the part of his mind arguing for caution. *It might be risky*, he thought, *but it's better than starving.*

David descended the last hill in front of the little settlement so as to come out on the road leading into it. It would look less suspicious for him to be seen arriving from a normal direction, rather than overland. When he reached the first of the tents and shacks that were the miners' dwellings, it seemed that his stomach's point of view was correct. No one paid him the least attention, and those who did look up as he passed looked back to their fry pans just as quickly.

David located a log structure that grandiosely proclaimed itself to be the "Emporium of the Golden West." In crudely lettered script it offered "Fine Merchandise and Choice Provender." The building was crowded with miners who were devouring plates of flapjacks in sorghum and clamoring for more. Scraps of overheard conversation informed David that this camp was new, only a month old at most, and owed its founding to a new gold strike.

A short, fat man wearing round spectacles on his round face was delivering orders in a high-pitched voice to a line of waiters carrying the heaping platters. David took him to be the owner, or at least the manager, and approached him to ask about supplies. He waited patiently for the torrent of instructions to subside.

"Jed, watch out for that jug."

"Seth, mind that you collect another dollar from that party by the door."

"Mose, bring some more coffee."

"No need to ask about a place, sit down anywhere and you'll be served."

David didn't even realize that the last comment was directed toward him till he saw the round little man waiting for him to be seated.

"No, no, I'm not interested in breakfast. That is, I am interested, but what I came in for is supplies," David stammered.

The proprietor looked him over and shook his head. "No time till after this rush subsides. Sit down and eat, if you've a mind to—dollar a plate and free coffee. I'll see to the rest presently." Before David could reply, he was back to shouting orders at the waiters.

Eventually the pace of flapjack consumption slowed, and David, who had never stopped glancing over his shoulder, had managed to eat a plate as well. Here and there a few individuals were still finishing breakfast, but only one table full of men remained, calling loudly for more.

The rotund little man bustled over. "Now sir, what supplies were you wanting?"

"I want to get outfitted with as much in the way of staple goods as this will purchase," said David, standing and removing the pouch from his belt.

"To be sure. To be sure. You are just newly arrived, then?" David thought he saw one of the men at the crowded table looking at him. "No, no, been here right along. Doing well, too."

The proprietor puckered his eyebrows above the round spectacles. "Curious that I haven't seen you before. This is the only store in these parts."

"Yes, well, can you get on with it?" David asked. The man who had been staring at him leaned over to whisper something to his neighbor. David couldn't decide whether it was best to turn away from their view or to continue standing so as to keep an eye on them.

"Let's just see your purchasing power," said the store-keeper, setting up scales. He poured David's pouch of gold into one pan, then began adding brass weights to the other.

"Say, where did you get this?" he asked in what

seemed to David an unnecessarily loud voice.

"I told you, I've been in the diggings for a while," said David nervously.

"But this gold didn't come from around these parts. This is real fine gold and everything we've seen here so far is coarse stuff. Where'd you say your claim was located?"

David saw the four men who had been seated at the table push back their chairs and start to stand. Hastily grabbing the pan, David poured the gold dust back into the leather pouch, spilling some on the counter. "That's all right. I've changed my mind."

"What's your rush?" asked the storekeeper.

"Your name Bollin?" growled a voice behind him.

David reached his hand under his sweater to grasp the butt of the derringer. When he made no reply, the man who had stepped up behind him laid a rough hand on his shoulder.

"I said, what's your name, stranger?"

David couldn't wait any longer. He spun around with the open pouch of gold dust in one hand, spraying its contents into the face of his challenger, and drawing the pistol with his other hand as he turned.

The startled ruffian put his hands up to his face as the glimmering powder hit him in the eyes, blinding him. "What the—?" he demanded, falling back a pace.

The sunlight streaming in through the slit windows of the log building turned the shower of gold into a cloud of shimmering sparks. The other three men stood transfixed for a moment, then froze as they noted the .44 caliber opening of the derringer pointed at them.

"I want a horse and I want it now," demanded David, glancing at the proprietor.

"Out back, tied to the tree. Take it, take it," the man stammered nervously, holding his pudgy hands in plain view.

"First one who tries to stop me will have a hole big enough to put his fist into," announced David, backing out the door. As soon as he set foot on the ground outside, he turned and ran for the rear of the building. A jumble of voices and a stamp of boots told him they were coming after him.

The storekeeper had told the truth. Tied to a limb of an oak tree was a short, dark-coated horse. David pulled on the rope to release it, just as the first pursuer rounded the corner of the building. He fired the derringer. The pistol, now loaded with birdshot, sprayed the side of the structure and peppered the man, who fell back yelling, "I've been hit!"

That single shot gave David the time he needed to jump on the horse's back and yank it around by the lead rope. He had no saddle or bridle, but David clung desperately to its mane and pounded away up the street.

The leader of the pursuers, still trying to rub gold dust out of his eyes, was shouting for the others to bring their horses around. His partner was pleading for someone to help him pick the bird shot out of his cheek and neck.

Ignoring them both, the storekeeper rushed behind the bar and picked up a dustpan and brush. Methodically he began to sweep up the golden specks scattered across the floor.

The horse David was riding had surely been born from the marriage of a mule and a sledgehammer. It was a good thing that the little black horse was headed up the road that led out of town, because no amount of pulling or sawing on the lead rope could turn the animal one inch. All David could do was hang on as tightly as possible; the horse seemed determined to stamp each leg down with as much force as possible.

The road led up an incline to the face of a steep hill, then began to circle the slope, still gaining in altitude all the time. David and the horse left the mining town behind, flashing past the last of the tents and huts. The ground to the right dropped off into another boulder-choked canyon. When David found that he was looking down on the tops of oak trees, he leaned over the left shoulder of the horse, pressing as close to the canyon wall as possible.

The black horse dug up chunks of earth from the trail without showing the least sign of becoming winded. As David looked around for a path or gully that he could use to escape the main trail, the sound of a shot echoed up the canyon and reverberated off the granite walls.

Throwing a quick glance around, David could see three riders coming up the trail after him. Even as he watched, the man on the lead horse extended his arm and a puff of smoke arose. A second crash resounded in the arroyo, then another.

David ducked low over the horse's withers, hugging as close to its compact neck as he could and wrapping his arms around its throat. A shot whizzed past, drawing a spark and a handful of dust from a rock just to the left of the trail.

He had almost reached the crest of the hill. The trail was flattening out, and David could see the area opening up into a small valley scattered with snow-covered oak trees and gooseberry bushes. If he could top the rise without getting shot, he stood a chance of getting into cover before the pursuers had time to finish their climb.

The trail made a sharp hairpin turn just a few yards from the top. David looked back over his shoulder again to see how close the followers were getting.

Just in the middle of the turn, some shale rock was hidden under the thin snow. As the black planted a pile-driver foot and began to turn his body, the hoof slid out from under him, and he lurched to the left.

The horse hit hard on his left shoulder. As the horse stumbled and its rear pitched up, David lost his grip. He executed a perfect somersault in the air, turning completely over and landing heavily on his back with a thud. The blow was cushioned by the layer of snow, but it still knocked the wind out of him and left him dazed.

The black rolled completely over, but came up again a dozen yards away, apparently unharmed, trailing its lead-rope in the snow. David shook his head as he rose shakily to his feet. He stumbled over the snow toward the black, hoping to grab its rope and swing back aboard.

As his hand reached out to grasp the rope, another shot was fired that threw up snow beneath the horse's belly. The beast plunged sideways, and the three riders galloped around the switchback as David's horse skittered over to an oak tree and stopped again.

David drew himself up and turned to face the pursuers. Two split off to circle him, cutting off his escape. The third halted with his horse facing David. He was the leader, still blinking furiously, his eyes watering from the gold dust.

"Bollin, we can take you back alive or slung over the

back of that black horse. It makes me no never-mind."

"Why don't you shoot me, then?" said David with more calm than he really felt.

"Don't rush me. You'd be a whole lot less trouble thataway, but Barton says he'd prefer you alive."

————

His hands tied together, David was placed back on the black horse and his feet bound underneath its belly. If he slid off again, he would certainly be trampled to death.

The posse started back down the slope at a walking pace. The man who had spoken was in the lead, and the other two rode flanking David and slightly behind.

"Where are you taking me?" David called to the leader.

"Back to Hangtown, of course. Barton aims to see that you get a fair trial before you're hanged. Ain't that right, boys?" This blunt jest sent the other two men into gales of laughter.

"Barton'll prob'ly figger to sell tickets," returned one.

"You bet," responded the leader. "Why, shoot, Bollin, if you dance real purty on the rope, Barton'll no doubt cut you in on the take!" More howls of laughter erupted from the three.

"You know I didn't mean to kill him," said David. "It was an accident."

The leader turned to look over his shoulder at David as he spoke. "It don't matter. Ain't nobody misses Moffat anyhow. You just stuck yore nose in where it din't belong. Why'd you try and help that old Chink, anyways?"

David was silent for a long time, and the leader continued to look at him curiously. "I guess it was just time for me to start doing what I knew was right."

"Well, savin' that short Chinee is gonna help you to a real long neck," returned the man, and he straightened back around in his saddle. At that moment the four riders were passing beneath a twelve-foot granite boulder that loomed over the trail like a stone idol brooding above the canyon. A gunshot erupted from the top of the rock, sounding as if a clap of thunder had burst right above their heads. At the same instant, David's horse gave a sudden scream that cut the morning stillness with such pain and terror that David felt as if a knife had been plunged into his chest.

The black horse fell over on its side and lay still for a moment. Its corpse then began a slow slide down into the canyon, dragging David's bound form along with it. Lying on the uphill side of the horse, he did not have his leg pinned beneath it, but the rope connecting his ankles still prevented him from being able to get away from the carcass.

The skid began to pick up speed as the slope increased; ahead lay the lip of a dropoff into a hundred-foot crevice. David hadn't even glanced toward this rapidly approaching danger. All his attention was focused on hugging as tightly as possible to the body of the horse. Gunshots tore into the ground near him, and one struck him in the thigh, making him cry out.

The other three riders had drawn their guns and were returning fire toward the top of the rock. They had not yet caught a glimpse of the attacker. As they began shooting back, the unseen marksman seemed to notice them for the first time. One of the riders, shot through the neck, fell dead from his horse. His animal bolted down the canyon trail, causing the leader's horse to rear and spin. The leader was thrown from the horse's back, and as more gunshots turned his way, he lunged over the edge of the path to shelter himself behind some small rocks lining its border.

The third member of the posse had prudently stepped from his mount, keeping its body between him and the source of the gunshots. He fired across his horse's back, his shots throwing up rock splinters from the top of the boulder and drawing a cry of pain from the attacker.

There was a lull in the firing. The two remaining men on the trail kept their Colts aimed toward the location from which the shots had come. The leader called out to the other, "Try to flank him! I'll make him keep his head down."

"Who's up there?" returned the other. "If he was trying to rescue Bollin, he came near to killing him right off instead!"

David was in a precarious spot. The black horse's body was resting right on the edge of the dropoff, on the verge of plunging over. Trying to get free of its dead weight, David crawled carefully backward over its rump, pulling the rope that tied his feet along the body in little jerks and bumps. The young man gritted his teeth against the pain of the leg wound. He was hidden by the steepness of the slope from any more shots from the rock above the trail. But looking upward toward the gun battle, David could see that the leader of the posse was watching his efforts to free himself as if debating whether to shoot David himself.

The rope hung up on something under the horse. David was completely behind the body, but couldn't free himself. He could feel its weight starting to shift again, moving almost imperceptibly toward the drop. In desperation, David threw himself backward with all the force he could achieve. The movement was too great for the remaining balance, and the body of the black horse plunged into the canyon.

In the moment of falling, its head and withers dropped over a split second before the hindquarters followed. The corpse slightly pivoted, and at the point when its eight-hundred pound weight should have carried David into the abyss, its legs pulled through the loop of rope.

David lay clutching two handfuls of gravel, his eyes screwed tightly shut. He had expected to be whizzing through the air to be crushed against the stony bottom of the arroyo. He lay completely still for a moment, not believing that the danger had dropped away and left him alive.

When it dawned on him that he was not lying in the depths of the canyon, he sat upright and began working with jerking motions of his bound hands to untie the rope from around his legs. Dark blood slowly seeped through the leg of his pants. Looking up toward the trail again, he could see the leader of the posse watching him intently. Suddenly, the man made up his mind.

"Bollin's gettin' loose!" he shouted, rising to his feet. "Hold it, Bollin," he ordered, "or I'll plug you right where you lay."

At the shout of David's name, the figure of Captain Greaves stood up on top of the monolith. A bullet from the second man's .45 hit Greaves squarely in the chest, and a flower of bright red blood blossomed instantly on the front of the sea captain's shirt.

As he crumpled to the ground, the pistol in Greaves'

hand discharged one final time. He had risen to his feet, seeking to aim another shot at David, but his shot found a different target. His bullet hit the leader of the posse right between the shoulder blades, and the man pitched forward over the slope. He rolled past David, tumbling head over heels down the rocky hillside. For one terrifying second it seemed that this additional falling body would strike David and carry him over the edge after all, but at the last instant, the rolling corpse veered aside and dropped like a stone into the canyon.

David succeeded in freeing himself from the rope around his ankles. He stood up, testing his leg, and began stumbling along the edge of the dropoff, limping down the canyon. His hands, still bound, were clasped in front of him as if in a continual attitude of prayer for deliverance. That was, in fact, what David was thinking.

The sole remaining member of the posse saw him running down the canyon. "Hold it, Bollin!" he shouted. When David didn't stop, the man leveled his pistol at David's retreating back and pulled the trigger. It clicked on an empty chamber. He thumbed the hammer back and tried again, without success.

By now David was out of sight along the bends of the arroyo. The man swung up on his mount and rode along the path. He caught one more glimpse of David, now far below him, angling down the slope. The man looked over the shale of the slope below the trail and considered the distance to the bottom of the canyon. "I'll be hanged if I'll risk my neck going down there," he muttered to himself. "Come on horse," he observed out loud, "let's go back to town."

————

The surviving member of the posse returned to the settlement known simply as The Forks. He went back to the general store and eating house that had been the scene of their early morning encounter with David.

Outside the store he found the comrade whose face had intercepted the birdshot fired by the derringer. The man's head was bound up in a bandage that ran over his hair and around his chin. This wrapping, along with the puffy, inflamed flesh that protruded from the bandage, made him look like a child with the mumps.

The bandaged man waved to his friend, and even tried to call out to him, although the effort of moving his face evidently caused him great pain. "Sandy, come here quick."

"What is it, Jim? Be glad you weren't along on this ride. Ned's dead; so's Billy. Some crazy man shot us up, and Bollin got clean away."

"But Sandy, Sandy, listen!" mumbled the other. The cloth wound around his face muffled his words.

"Yessir," Sandy continued, "killed 'em both stone dead. I nailed him, or he'd a prob'ly got me too."

By now the bandaged man was fairly jumping up and down in his efforts to make his friend listen. "Shut up, you fool!" he fairly shouted, then groaned and put a hand up to his jaw as the stretched cheek had a sudden spasm.

Three men stepped out the front door of the store, all armed and wearing serious expressions.

"Are you Sandy Sullivan?" demanded a tall brown-haired man, laying a hand on the butt of his revolver.

"Well now, maybe I am, and maybe I ain't," answered Sandy with a sneer. "Depends on who's askin'."

The brown-haired man drew his Colt and held the barrel against Sandy's chest. "That's good enough for me," he replied. "I'm Cobb, newly elected sheriff of the Hangtown Mining District. These are my deputies," he added, nodding toward the others who also stood in poses of readiness for battle. "I've got a warrant for your arrest, as an accomplice of Barton."

Sandy's jaw dropped and his mouth hung open. "I tried to tell you, Sandy," mumbled Jim. "Tried to warn you."

"What do you mean, 'accomplice'? Barton is the head of the committee that runs Hangtown!"

"Not any more," continued Cobb smoothly. "Not since Widow Parker recognized Barton from a wanted poster back in St. Joe. Man name of Morris is head of the committee now. Seems he knew Barton from Frisco, where Moffat and Barton were both wanted in connection with a murder."

"That's got nothing to do with me," blustered Sandy. "We was just followin' orders to bring in Bollin for murderin' Moffat."

"Yeah, and it's a good thing you didn't kill him, because you'd be looking at a murder charge yourself."

"How do you figure that?" asked Sandy, glaring sullenly.

"The new committee has brought in a verdict of death by misadventure; Bollin is innocent!"

CHAPTER 14

David struggled up the steep slope on the opposite side of the canyon from the gun battle. Pausing to gasp for breath, he scanned the hillside below him and the trail across from him for signs of renewed pursuit. Seeing no indication of anyone close behind, David took the time to work on the knot of the rope that bound his hands. He tugged the coarse hemp with his teeth, forcing himself to keep trying even as the rough fibers pulled and cut into his wrists.

Once his hands were free, David examined the damage to his leg. He winced as he pulled the fabric of the trousers away from the wound. The bullet had passed completely through without shattering the bone. The holes had not bled much, in spite of the exertion of climbing out of the gorge. David continued to stagger on toward the top of the ridge.

He had a destination in mind. He had seen Greaves at the moment the captain was shot. There was no mistaking the leaping gush of blood from Greaves' chest. Since civilization was closed to David, he would go back to the dead man's hideout and remain there until he could come up with another plan, some way to get home.

He stumbled over the crest of the hill. Looking back at the little settlement, David felt a sense of regret and longing. He knew that he would find no aid in any of the mining towns. Nor could he endanger Keo, Strawfoot, or Ling Chow, even if he had a way to get a message to them. He would have to go it alone and survive as best he could in the secluded arroyo camp.

David made his way back up the stream bed he had followed when leaving the hideout. The snow had melted, and treacherous muddy footing remained in its place. He crossed the stream several times in an attempt to cover his trail, leaping from rock to rock. The impact of each landing made him clutch his leg in pain.

David was still wearing the waterproof raingear he had taken from the hideout, but he had lost the faithful derringer.

Afternoon stretched into evening before David managed to reach the narrow, boulder-choked length of canyon marking the lower end of the creek's outlet from the hidden valley. He knew he would have to climb out of the canyon again and descend Greaves' secret cable to return to the cabin. This was all too much for his exhausted condition and the early darkness. Finding a sheltered place in the rocks, the fugitive curled up and went to sleep.

———

Torrential rains and a bitterly cold north wind swept over the high Sierras, obscuring the blue peaks from view.

William Bollin, accompanied by Keo, strode into the log shack that now served Hangtown as jail and sheriff's office. The sheriff looked at them from his bunk. He did not attempt to rise.

Sullivan and Barton were imprisoned with half a

dozen other men in a space ten-by-ten feet square. The new sheriff made his office in the outer area. There was room for a small stove, a bunk, and a chair. An upturned crate served as both desk and table, and a deck of cards sat ready for a game of poker played between prisoners and the sheriff.

Through a narrow slit in the heavy wooden cell door, Barton mocked, "Well if it isn't the holy saint Reverend Bollin and his Kanaka dog out for a stroll!"

The sheriff responded by hurling a boot at the slit, which sent Barton momentarily ducking from his peephole. A great round of laughter and curses resounded in the tiny prison.

"You'd best shut up, Barton." The sheriff sat up slowly. "These fellas are bringin' your supper, and I wouldn't blame 'em if they et it theirselves." Now silence fell behind the door.

Keo placed a large cloth-covered box on the floor beside the stove. The aroma of biscuits and beans and fried chicken was unmistakable.

"Widow Parker says this supper enough for ten men. You eat first. Mince pie for you."

The sheriff was already pawing through the basket and making smacking noises with his lips as several pairs of eyes now crowded to stare through the slit.

William Bollin cleared his throat, but the sheriff did not look up until he found the pie and held it up for all to see.

"Keo and I would like to go with you to retrieve the bodies of the dead men. And to look for my son," he said quietly. "When will we leave?"

Sheriff Cobb inhaled the aroma of the chicken and rummaged for a drumstick. "We won't be goin' anywheres until the weather clears, Parson. It ain't worth dyin' of pneumony to fetch a load of dead men."

"But my son—" Bollin protested. "Barton's man said he was still alive."

The sheriff bit off a mouthful of chicken and shook his head. "He won't be alive when we find him, Parson. Not meanin' to discourage you none, but he ain't gonna live through the night. Not with weather like this. He was all trussed up, scramblin' down a path no wider than chicken tracks. And no food. Give it up, Parson. Say your prayers for him and get on with your life. Your boy ain't gonna be found alive."

Keo and Kapono Bollin exchanged glances of indignation and concern at the sheriff's disregard for David. A chorus of hoots and laughter emanated from the cell. Someone howled out, "When the roll is called up yonder, he'll be there!"

Keo looked as angry and dark as the storm that raged outside. Kapono Bollin put a hand on his arm to calm him.

"Keo and I will bring back the bodies of the dead men. Save you the trouble, Sheriff." William Bollin's voice was amazingly matter-of-fact. "We will need a map showing the exact location. And horses."

The sheriff shrugged. "Sure. Whatever you want." A fresh gale of wind moaned over the little building. Sheriff Cobb looked up toward the rafters as if beseeching God. "But you ain't gonna find your boy alive. If I thought different, I'd go with you. But it ain't likely."

"Don't let them go, Sheriff," wailed a prisoner in mock concern. "You'll end up picking up two more dead men!"

A chicken bone bounced against the door. "All right,

Sandy Sullivan! These gentlemen'll be needin' a map. A good map, if you please, or you ain't getting none of this fine supper!"

Silence fell over the group behind the door. "Sure," came Sandy's muffled reply. "But don't blame me if these fools freeze to death and don't get back!"

"I'll blame you!" shouted Sheriff Cobb. "And you ain't gonna eat ever again if you don't draw the exact map." He shoved a scrap of paper beneath the door and dropped a pencil through the slot. "Make it quick and be warned!" he menaced.

What had been a trail before the rains was now little more than a faint track fit only for mountain goats.

Keo rode a stout black mare that had belonged to one of Barton's men. Two sure-footed pack mules followed behind him, then William Bollin on a mountain-bred bay mare, leading another mule at the tail of the procession. "This path bad as Waipio, eh Kapono Bollin?" Keo called over his shoulder as the track all but disappeared along the steep canyon wall.

William nodded and looked up at the sheer rock face that rose another five hundred feet above them. Not a single tree or shrub clung to the sides of the gorge. Only a series of sharp switchbacks marred the nearly perpendicular wall that climbed to a dizzying height above the bottom of the gorge.

When they had climbed three quarters of the way along a path, measuring a mere thirty inches wide in places, the ledge grew even more narrow and dangerous. One wrong step meant certain death for men and animals. William looked down at the barren trees on the floor of the gorge. After half a lifetime in the perpetual summer of his island home, the pastor had forgotten the barren landscape of impending winter. He shuddered involuntarily as he prayed for his son, who had never known the bitter winds of this season. Could David survive?

Sheriff Cobb had offered a fourth pack mule. "You may be carryin' home one more over the saddle, Parson," he had said.

William had simply shook his head and told the pessimistic lawman that David could ride back to town behind him.

Rocks and gravel slid away beneath the hoofs of Keo's mount as she scrambled and strained to gain footing on the switchback corner above William. The sand pelted William, and for a moment he thought that Keo's horse would fall over and wipe all of them from the ledge in one sweep.

Keo looked fearfully over the edge and called down, "Very bad, Kapono. You pray plenty!"

William nodded. *The steps of a good man are ordered by the Lord, and he delighteth in his way. Though he fall. . . .* Keo's horse jumped forward over the loose shale. A fresh downpour of gravel pelted the end mule, causing it to balk momentarily and pull back on William's lead rope. *He shall not be utterly cast down.* The bay mare scrambled upward, attempting to gain footing on the upper level of the switchback. The earth fell away beneath her rear legs, and rocks ricocheted off the wall of the gorge.

"Kapono Bollin!" Keo shouted and urged his own horse farther forward to give the struggling bay more room. Her neck bowed forward, straining against the pull of the valley floor. William prayed for help as he felt the horse losing the battle. He stood forward in the stirrups until his head was over hers. Forelegs pawed and dug in the sliding ground. Back legs struck at rock and soil, finding no hold. Could the search end this way?

"YOUR HAND, LORD!" William cried out. "GIVE . . . US YOUR . . . HAND!"

In that instant, the horse lunged forward while the pack mule screamed and fell away into the abyss. Within seconds the mare stood trembling on the narrow ledge. Shaken, but safe.

Somehow Keo had managed to dismount. He peered wide-eyed around the black mare, then he looked down and down to where the end pack mule finally tumbled onto a boulder. Keo did not speak. He could not. Death was very near them now. Above them three bodies lay still and cold. Below them a terrible force seemed determined to drag them to their deaths.

"I am all right," Kapono Bollin said in a calm and quiet voice. "Do not be afraid, Keo. I felt His hand. He is with us. He is with us."

At that, William swung carefully off his frightened mount, easing his way forward until he stood in front of her. "Easy now," he soothed her, stroking her foam-flecked neck. "We must lead them on foot, Keo," he called. "And the Lord will lead us!"

If the trail up the crumbling switchback was frightening, the scene that awaited the travelers beside the monolith of granite was stark, grim horror. Rain had mingled with the blood spilled on top of and around the rock's base, until the stone resembled an ancient altar of human sacrifice. The man shot through the neck was lying face up in the trail, exactly where he had fallen. The blood that had drained his life away had pooled under his body. Sheltered there from the rain, it formed a ghostly image of the man's form that remained even after his corpse had been loaded onto the pack mule.

Leaning carefully over the precipice and looking far down into the gorge, Keo could just barely make out a flash of red from the bandanna tied around the throat of another body.

"Kapono Bollin," said Keo, "I can work my way down to body there." He pointed over the edge. "You stay here and check for man on top of rock?"

"Of course," replied the pastor. "And you be careful, Keo. There are enough bodies in this canyon already."

Keo removed a coil of rope they had brought for this purpose and tied it securely around a rock. Then he began to make a sliding, cautiously controlled descent.

William Bollin worked his way around the standing stone. He discovered a way to climb to its high side, then picked his way over a heap of rubble till at last he came out on its pinnacle. Face down before him lay the body of a man dressed in the dark blue dungarees and foul weather gear of a sailor. The corpse looked curiously flat, crumpled into the rocky surface as if it had tried to melt into a crevice of the stone with only partial success.

Swallowing hard, Pastor Bollin rolled the body over. The shirt, which should have been white, was dyed a deep reddish-brown, much like the color of the soil of the hillside from which the boulder thrust.

The preacher stood for several minutes, searching for some sign of David on the hills. Keo struggled again to the lip of the arroyo. He had a third body slung over his shoulder, which he held there with the pressure of one hand, while with the other he kept a tight grip on the rope. The Hawaiian lunged forward for one more pull and staggered onto the trail. He rolled the body from his shoulder onto the ground, then sat down panting for a minute.

When Keo stood up, he called to William. "Kapono Bollin!" He paused to catch his breath before resuming, "Kapono Bollin, you all right?"

"Yes," came the reply from above. "There is another dead man up here, just like that outlaw said."

"You wait," called the native. "I come help." He scrambled up to join the pastor on the summit of the rock.

"Hey," Keo puffed, "I know this man. This Captain Greaves, whale ship captain for Kawika and me."

William Bollin straightened up and looked grimly over the unending series of mountains and valleys that fell away from this place. David was somewhere out there. But where? The highest peaks were already white with snow. The spruce and pine of the lower mountains were dusted white. The pall of winter death seemed everywhere.

These three dead men were just a small remnant of a multitude whose lives had been shattered by the lust for gold. Bollin remembered the words of the bartender in San Francisco: *They sold their souls for the golden calf. . . .* " He glanced at the three bodies. What good were all the riches of the Sierras to them now?

William sighed and shook away the ominous thought that it might also be too late for David.

The lifeless forms were tied securely to the remaining

pack animals. Only then did Kapono Bollin share his thoughts with the Hawaiian.

"I am staying here, Keo," he said in a low voice. "David was here, right here, not long ago."

Keo glanced doubtfully at the lowering sky. "Big gale coming, Kapono Bollin. I see such storms on the ocean. Big wind. Plenty snow to freeze off a man's fingers on the rigging. You come back now. You not find Kawika in this world."

William put his hand on the broad shoulder of Keo. "I must search for him, Keo. If he is alive, he will need help. If he is dead . . ." His voice trailed away and his eyes lingered on a single shaft of sunlight that broke through the clouds and rested on the bald dome of a distant peak.

Keo pulled a thick canvas tarp from one of the bodies, then unstrapped a saddlebag full of provisions. "One week, Kapono Bollin." Keo furrowed his brow and narrowed his eyes as if he were speaking to a child. "You stay here one week. If you don't come back, Keo come back here. Iahova take six days to make all this, and then he rested. So. You look. I come for you on the seventh day."

William Bollin nodded his agreement, grasped the hand of Keo in farewell, and began his search even before the sound of hoofbeats had died away.

———

It had been three full days since David had eaten. His wounded leg ached. The world shimmered in his fevered vision. He had traveled less than four miles, and now he wandered in hopeless confusion. Once David had fallen down to rest, and when he had awakened he thought he was in Hawaii again. Pitifully, he called out for his friend Edward, and then for his father. *"I have fallen from the Pali, Father,"* he breathed, raising his face from the gravel. *"And I am lost."*

He lay weeping, like a child who had wandered from home. Would no one come for him? Would no one find him until it was too late?

With that thought, David jerked his head up. *Now he remembered!* If they found him they would kill him. And if he remained here for one more night, he would certainly die from the cold and the hunger that ravaged him.

He squeezed his eyes tightly shut and shook his head to clear his vision. He said his own name aloud. He wanted to pray, to ask God for help, but words seemed beyond reach.

Suddenly, he heard his own voice whisper a verse he had memorized years before as his father had taught him the story of another David who had fled to the wilderness from King Saul. *"When my foot slippeth, they magnify themselves against me. For I am ready to halt, and my sorrow is continually before me."*

He lifted his eyes to the silent rocks and trees that surrounded him. Was someone watching him? Someone just beyond his blurred vision who stood behind the trees to watch and wait? David propped himself on his arm and looked desperately around for the presence he felt so near. "Where are you?" he shouted hoarsely. Then, once again he repeated the words of the Psalmist, *"I will be sorry . . . for my sin. . . . Oh God, help me,"* he finished quietly, bowing his head in exhaustion and grief. And then he slept.

———

David was uncertain how many hours he had passed in sleep. Or was it days? His head was clearer now. He pulled himself to a sitting position and looked around. Suddenly he recognized a dozen landmarks he had etched in his memory before leaving the hidden canyon. He was very near; he was certain of that now.

His eyes traced the down slope of a familiar ridge until it disappeared behind an enormous boulder. Yes. The canyon was just beyond that point. Safety and refuge was within walking distance. No longer confused, David wiped his dirt-caked face in relief.

David's leg had stiffened up considerably and the young man had to massage the muscles for several minutes before the limb felt flexible enough to walk on. Locating a forked branch to use as a crutch, he leaned heavily on it while moving toward the rim of Greaves' hidden canyon. In the gray afternoon of drifting mist, David could not find the rope that would let him enter the shelter he was so anxiously seeking. Crossing an expanse of slick shale, the tip of his improvised support slipped out from under his weight, dropping him heavily onto his injured leg.

David ground his teeth together and rocked back and forth, holding both hands over the throbbing wound. When at last the pain subsided, David raised up and spotted the crutch stuck in a clump of brush a little way down the slope.

Crawling forward to retrieve the stick, he slid down to it and found the tree stump that was the anchor for Greaves' lifeline. David laughed out loud. This was no coincidence. Had he not fallen, and had the crutch not lodged just where it did, he would have stumbled past the hidden cord and perhaps never found the way down.

He breathed a silent prayer of thanks and felt the kindly presence of the Watcher once again.

Descending the rope was a great struggle. Taking a loop of cable around his hands, he let it slip slowly through his fingers, while the boot-tip on his good leg groped for a support. More than once he hung suspended over the edge of the cliff before finding a tiny crack in the rock with the toe of his boot. His mind went back to the day he had dropped a knife over the edge of a high *Pali* on Oahu. Edward Hupeka had held the rope with his strong brown arms while David had descended to retrieve it. Now the laughing words of encouragement seemed to echo audibly in the canyon. Somehow he felt as if Edward stood above him, helping him safely down the granite wall an inch at a time.

When at last his feet touched the firm ground of the canyon, he called up, "Thank you, Edward! Thanks for your prayers!"

Was the momentary flash of a smile and the upraised arm only imagination? David squinted up to the rim of the canyon, his vision blurred again. He winced. Edward was not there, of course. *Imagination. Wishes.* David was alone.

He turned away and staggered painfully toward the little shack. Falling through the door, he threw himself on the rough cot and lay there until the world stopped spinning around him.

He eyed the cold hearth longingly. There could be no fire for warmth or cooking or light tonight. He dared not give in to such a luxury. A single wisp of smoke could lead his pursuers to this place.

His gaze wandered to the rock shelf where Greaves had stacked provisions. Tins of hardtack and crackers were there, along with coffee, beans, and flour.

"*Maikai*," David whispered as he closed his eyes to sleep. "It is good."

Something roused David at midnight. He had been having a dream of home, the little church where he had grown up. He saw the figure of his father standing at the pulpit, his arms spread wide to embrace them all.

In his dream he saw Mary seated across the aisle, giving him a shy smile before turning her pretty features back toward Kapono Bollin.

His father was asking them to stand and sing, and as they did the booming voice of the preacher led out, "All Hail the Power of Jesus' Name." In the vision, David could hear the words clearly, "*Po-ni ia Iesu ke 'Lii mau.* Crown Jesus Lord of all."

Flushed and confused, David walked outside into the chilly night air, trying to clear his muddled brain. The air seemed to carry a faint echo of the refrain from his dream. *I must be feverish*, he thought.

Far off in the night sky and low against the horizon, an orange star suddenly appeared. It grew in brightness and intensity. David stood in wonder at the sight until his brain finally sounded the alarm. *It's a watch fire*, he thought. *It means they're still after me.*

David went quickly back inside the cabin and shut the door. He lay shivering in the tarp, but sleep refused to return.

Suddenly his aching stomach reminded him that he was hungry. His need for food was stronger than his fear of being heard by some phantom pursuer in the dark.

Trying not to put weight on his wounded leg, David

crawled from beneath the tarp and groped his way across the hard-packed dirt floor toward the rock shelf.

Pulling himself up, he reached toward a heavy tin, his hands trembling as he took it from the ledge. He fumbled to open it and reached in eagerly. Then he cried out in disappointment as his fingers closed around a small rock. He sat down on the floor and dumped out the tin. It was filled with stones and rocks! David wept in frustration as he ran his fingers over the cold pebbles in the darkness. Captain Greaves seemed to mock him from the grave. *Which of you, if your son asks for bread, gives him a stone?*

It was a cruel joke from one dead man to another. Greaves had his revenge: David would also die if he did not eat soon. Weary and nearly overcome with despair, David clutched a handful of the stones and gritted his teeth in anger.

But something was wrong. The stones were cool and smooth, not hard and jagged like rocks. Still clutching the pebbles, he made his way to the cabin door and flung it open, letting in a blast of cold air.

In the dim light of the stars, the pebbles glinted. He opened his fist and held the handful of rocks close to his eyes. *Gold!* David laughed bitterly. So Greaves had struck it rich and had hidden his wealth in a hardtack tin!

But what good was any of it now? David could not eat it. It could not keep him warm or heal his wound. It could not give him life.

He closed the cabin door and let the nuggets slip through his fingers to the floor. Returning to the ledge, he reached for a second tin. It, too, was heavy.

He pried open the lid and stuck his fingers in—it was full to the brim with nuggets. With a cry of desperation,

David let it fall with a clatter to the ground. He reached out for the third tin with the plea, "*Father? Just one slice of bread. Oh please!*"

The third tin was lighter. He shook it hesitantly; it rattled. David carefully opened the lid and reached in. *Crackers?* He raised it to his nose and inhaled reverently. *Soda crackers! Bread!*

He laughed and cried in gratitude as he raised a small, salty square to his lips and held it between his teeth for a moment before biting down.

Had he ever tasted anything so good? He took two more squares from the tin and returned it to the shelf, then carried his treasure back to the tarp.

For the remaining hours of darkness, David huddled beneath the canvas and nibbled on the crackers. When daylight came he would check his meager stores of food and calculate how long he could remain here and survive. The gold nuggets still lay scattered across the dirt floor.

CHAPTER 15

Pastor William Bollin had claimed all the mountains of the High Sierras for his King. For six days he climbed peaks and descended wild valleys in search of David.

He did not cry out the name of his son, but his booming voice resounded through the forest hymns and praises in the Hawaiian tongue.

Ho'o-ka-ni ke 'Lii mai-ka'i . . .
All hail the power of Jesus name!
Let angels prostrate fall . . .

If David were still alive, he would hear and recognize the voice of his father!

Song followed song. As drops of freezing rain clung to his beard and numbed his hands, he scrambled over slick rocks and cheered himself with song. *"Come, Thou Fount of every blessing! Iesu E, Kumu Nui!"*

The cold did not seem to pierce him. The chilling fear that time was running out for his son did not cause him to despair:

"All the way my Savior leads me! Iesu mau Ku'u . . . "

Every daylight hour was filled with searching and singing followed by a time of silent prayer and waiting for the voice of his son to call for him. But only the hushed whisper of the wind through the pines answered William Kapono Bollin.

At night he built a fire on the rock that towered over the maze of valleys. *Surely David will see the light and be drawn to its warmth*, he thought.

And so the six days and nights of hoping passed away without an answer. William ate a small morsel of hard-tack, then wrapped the remaining supply tightly and placed it inside the canvas shelter as the sound of Keo's horses drew near the camp.

He left enough food behind to sustain a man for three days. Kapono Bollin had fasted for that length of time, in hopes of having food left to care for David.

Now, as the sky spit out a stinging snow, Kapono Bollin left his hopes and his heart and rode wearily down to The Forks.

———

For a week David ate and slept well. In his waking hours, he distracted himself from the pain in his leg by rigging snares for birds and other small animals. These traps he constructed by pulling fibers from ropes. The pattern his fingers followed was learned in his childhood from Hawaiian acquaintances who used such devices in the mountainous valleys of their island home.

David's hands may have automatically carried out the braiding of the snares, but his conscious mind was carried back to island days spent with Edward and with Mary—and to memories of his father. David's father had always encouraged him to learn as much as possible from his Hawaiian friends. For a long time, David's boyhood had been an exciting life as the blond-haired child had played and learned with his darker companions. David found himself wondering when the life of the islands had ceased to satisfy him. He remembered the importance he had attached to the ambition to be wealthy, to be respected, to have a fine cultured home back in the States. How foolish that all seemed now.

When the day came that he felt he could give his wound no more time to heal, he set the snares in the woods on the top of the cliff. Catching no game that day, he put himself on half rations. Two more days passed until he finally caught a rabbit in one of the traps. He gave in and built a fire, and that night he splurged in celebration, devouring the rabbit and treating himself to another biscuit, baked rock-hard by the edge of the fire.

Two weeks passed with nothing in the snares. David's precious supplies dwindled away. Each day he allowed himself to eat less than the day before.

One morning David awoke at dawn to the sound of an icy rain falling in earnest. He wanted to ascend the cliff again to inspect his trapline, but could not. The cable and rockface were too slippery to support his climb. Reducing his rations still further, he waited out the storm by braiding more snares.

When the rain finally stopped, twenty-four hours had crept by. The feeble sunlight had barely changed the canyon's blackness to a gloomy gray before David was clambering up the rock wall. Once he slipped and almost fell, hanging on grimly while his toes groped for footing on the slick surface and his injured leg protested the abuse in a scream of pain.

David had inspected all the traps but the last two; all of them were empty. Then he came upon the remains of another rabbit. As if to taunt him, the fox that had beaten him to the kill left only the rabbit's head behind.

When the last trap also proved to be empty, David returned to the cabin and fixed himself a scanty meal of two scraps of fat bacon and another lump of flour. Then he lay down to sleep and tried to ignore the complaints of his stomach.

———

It was raining again; the storm was even stronger at the higher elevations. The trickle of water into the hidden chamber had filled the stone bowl until it overflowed, flooding half of the floor. David moved his meager provisions to a sheltered location, then began stacking his supply of firewood on the drier side of the cavern.

An hour later the rain slacked and stopped. He peered out and up toward the threatening sky. He would have to inspect his trap line. If he waited, the storm might begin again, perhaps isolating him in the cave for several days.

Bitter disappointment filled him as he went from snare to snare, finding each empty and untouched. It seemed as if David himself were the only living creature in the canyon. And without food he would die soon enough.

It started to rain again. The clouds lowered over the arroyo until the morning was almost as dark as night. David nearly broke off his examination of the remaining snares; to delay longer might trap him outside his shelter. *Besides*, he told himself, *there isn't going to be any game. This is a waste of time*.

But his stomach drove him to complete the circuit of the traps. The last snare was a tiny net of hemp, rigged from the leftover remains of the other traps and set in a low elderberry bush almost as an afterthought.

David shrugged as he passed the bush and turned back toward the canyon. The snare was empty, just as he had thought. He started to walk away, then turned again toward the bush. There was something caught in the trap! A shape a little darker and a little bulkier than the bush itself was hanging in the center of the fibers.

David moved cautiously toward the shrub. Even though there had been no movement, David's anxiety rose; he feared that whatever was caught there might break free and escape. He moved to stand beside the bush, then bent down to peer into its shadowed recess. Upside down, suspended from the woven snare, hung a quail.

Gently, even tenderly, David untangled the strands of hemp from the bird's legs. As he held it in his hands he was struck with the desire to tear it apart and stuff its flesh into his mouth. He struggled with this desperate compulsion for a few moments, then forced himself to place the bird inside the pocket of his raincoat.

He started to run back toward the shelter, but made himself slow down and walk for fear that he would fall on the rain-slick hillside and lose his prize. Every few steps he would pat his pocket to check that the tiny body was still in place, and twice he stopped and took the little carcass out and turned it over and over in his hands, marvelling at his good fortune.

Before starting down the cable he took a length of rope, cut it with his pocket knife, and looped it around the outside of his coat. He tied it in place over the pocket that contained the quail as extra protection against it somehow falling from the pocket as he was descending. The rain changed to lazily spinning white snowflakes and descended with him.

When he reached the cabin, David took the quail's tiny form and laid it on the stone sideboard. With his knife he began to whittle shavings to form into a pile in the fire pit. He started to rake out some live coals from the previous night's blaze to get his fire going again, but stopped to run over to the rocky ledge to check to see that the quail was still there. Then he returned to the fire, digging out the embers and piling on the shavings. He blew gently until the kindling sprang to life with a cheerful blaze.

When the fire was burning to suit him, he whittled a sharp point to the end of a long stick. He pictured himself reclining beside the fire as he cooked the bird to a golden brown, and his mouth began to water at the thought.

He retrieved the bird and settled himself by the fireside to pluck it, carefully pulling off each downy feather so as not to harm the skin beneath. When the tiny form was bare, he took his pocket knife and gutted the bird, then skewered it onto the stick and began to roast it over the flames.

Drops of fat began to ooze out and fall sizzling on the coals. David stopped cooking long enough to get a skillet in which to catch the drips. He took the skewered bird with him, afraid that it might fall into the fire and be ruined while he was away momentarily.

At last he couldn't stand to wait any longer, and he laid the tiny form into a puddle of its own grease in the skillet. With utmost care he began to dismember it with his knife. He took a minute slice of meat and popped it in his mouth, shutting his eyes and letting the morsel rest on his tongue before he began to chew.

Soon he was pulling off bigger chunks, and at last he thrust the entire ribcage into his mouth and started to chew it up bones and all. He tried to slow down but couldn't. He was devouring the bird, crunching its bones, swallowing sharp fragments that scratched his throat as he choked them down.

Soon it was all gone; all but the clawed feet. David picked up the fry pan and began to lick its surface, sucking every drop of grease from the metal. When he had finished, he put the skewer in his mouth and chewed the end of the stick to draw the last flavored drops from it.

His eye fell on the minuscule claws. He picked them up and nibbled on one speculatively. It was like eating wire or coarse brush. He decided that he would cut them up into small pieces and force himself to choke them down. He picked up the knife to hack at the tiny feet, when the gleam of firelight off the blade caught his eye.

David brought the knife up nearer to his face. Reflected in its shiny surface he saw his eye, but it was like no human eye he had ever seen before. It was bloodshot and sunken, and his eye sockets seemed to overhang his eyes as if his soul had retreated far inside his head. He turned the blade this way and that, catching glimpses of hollow cheeks, scraggly beard with patches missing, and unkempt strands of hair that hung down all around.

From the bed David stared woefully at the empty tins of provisions and the useless containers filled with Greaves' gold nuggets.

How he resented those tiny gold lumps which filled up space that might have held hardtack, crackers, or flour! David rolled over and stared at the moss-filled chinks in the cabin wall. He remembered the smooth hewn timbers of his father's house, the clean sheets, the fragrant warmth of the breezes that lulled him to sleep at night.

All the gold in the mountains could not buy those things for him now. And if he loaded his pockets full with the stuff and trekked back to The Forks to buy himself a meal, he would be captured and strung up.

As the penniless son of a missionary, David had been wealthier by far than he was now with handfuls of gold within his grasp. All those years he had been rich, but he never knew it until now. Tears stung his eyes as he thought of his father and those dear friends he had turned his back on. He longed to see them just one more time. He ached to tell them how wrong he had been.

Perhaps a letter? But there was not even a scrap of paper in the cabin. David frowned. He could remain here only a short time. His scant provisions would be gone by the end of the week and then he would have to rely on his trap line. Death by starvation seemed a certainty. He wondered if anyone would ever find this place, find his body and wonder at the horde of useless gold.

They would not even know his name. They would not care enough to bury him.

He sat up slowly and reached for his knife and a smooth bit of firewood. He would carve his own name, the name of his father and their address in Hawaii. Perhaps a verse—some message that might be sent home that his father might know that David had died loving him.

For hours he worked, carefully carving out his name and that of his father:

DAVID, SON OF REV. WILLIAM BOLLIN
MISSION BOARD,
HONOLULU, OAHU

What message could he leave so that his heart would be somehow read and understood? How could he say, "*Like the Prodigal son, I would have come home . . .*"?

David winced as the pain of longing filled his heart. He could not remember the scripture reference for the story of the Prodigal. He had never liked the story or even understood it until now. He wished he had paid more attention. He wished he had a Bible to read. But such wishing was useless, and so he carved out the sweet words that had comforted him when he stood before his mother's grave.

ORA LOA IA IESU

Endless life by Jesus. Even as he etched the words, he found comfort in them. He was carving his own epitaph, and suddenly he was no longer afraid to die. He had died here already. All the empty things he once thought important now seemed foolish—as foolish and useless as the gold nuggets in the hardtack tin.

David smiled for the first time in months. He was free. He could see his father clearly, and he loved what he saw.

In that moment David also saw clearly what he must do. Somehow he must leave this place and find a way to tell his father what he had discovered in his heart. He could not trust such a message to a carved piece of firewood and a chance that someone might someday discover his remains.

David closed his eyes. Tomorrow morning he would head back to The Forks and turn himself in. Surely they would let him live long enough to write the words . . .

CHAPTER 16

Snow fell all night, and morning only changed the swirling gray curtain to one of white, a wet snow that blew against the sides of trees and rocks and clung there. The storm was blowing in out of the west, on a rising wind. Anyone who had spent a winter in the Sierras would have instantly recognized the signs of a blizzard. But David had never spent a winter in the Sierras, never seen a real snowfall.

The thin dusting of powder through which he had hiked on his earlier trip to The Forks was nothing like this. Whole clumps of icy dampness struck David squarely in the face. The snow stuck to his beard and the hair that protruded from his hat. He had to tuck his mouth down into the collar of the coat so as not to get a mouthful of snow while trying to breathe.

David had to wipe the snow from his eyes every few paces so he could peer ahead into the billowing particles. When leaving the canyon hideout, he had firmly fixed in his mind the direction of the watchfire he had seen. He told himself that to go there in as direct a line as possible was best. To find where men had been was to find men, and the food he desperately needed. What he had not counted on was that once outside the narrow confines of the little arroyo, even the smallest distances became vast. David's goals shrank from the next ridgeline, to the next tall pine, to the next boulder, dimly seen only a dozen feet away.

In a partly sheltered hollow David saw the tops of some plant stalks. From some hidden corner of his mind he pulled out the knowledge that these were lily stalks, and that at their roots he might find a bulb that could be eaten. Eagerly he kicked aside the snow, dug into the earth, and probed with his hands. He pried up a handful of tiny bulbs and crunched on them. He could not have said if they had any flavor, just as he could not have said whether he had learned of them from Strawfoot or Keo or Ling Chow or his father.

The small patch was soon exhausted, and David plunged on again, out of the protected place into a drift five feet deep. He floundered there for a while, trying to push his way straight ahead into a snowbank that seemed to get higher and higher until it rose above his head. At the same time it seemed to grow softer underfoot, as if the whole world had turned to snow and he was swimming in the middle of it.

At last he could go no farther forward. He turned around to try to retrace his steps, only to find that the passage he had forced with such great effort had already closed in behind him. He turned round and round in place, unable to go forward, unwilling to fight the same battle over again to go back. *Will I freeze to death standing up here?* he wondered. He started to climb up over the snowbank. At its rim he lay down on his stomach and crawled like a great wounded beast. When his outstretched arms encountered a tree trunk, he clung to it, feeling like the snow would suck him back down if he let go.

After a time he pulled himself around to the other side of the tree. He had reached a hillside that sloped upward away from the swale where he had nearly smothered in snow. He began to pull himself up the slope from branch to branch. How high above the ground he was walking, he could not say, but he stepped gingerly, testing each foothold, expecting at any moment to fall through into a final resting place in a column of snow.

His strength was failing. He was badly in need of food. Shelter would be wonderful, warmth would be paradise, but food was a necessity. The fires of his body's furnace were burning low. Without food soon, the machinery that placed one aching foot in front of another would cease to function.

David could not have known by sight or any difference in the feel of the snow underfoot that he was on the crest of a hill. Instead, that sensation came to him as snowflakes suddenly seemed to be blowing upward into his face. There was a lifting quality to the wind, almost as if he and the snow might be lifted up and blown back skyward.

He fell over a mound of rocks, picked himself up, and immediately fell over another. As he fell, he rolled sideways into a slanting expanse of snow-covered stone. The white-draped wall he took to be stone yielded under his weight. It gave beneath him, and when he rolled off, it sprang back.

Rubbing the snow from his eyes and shaking loose the wet clumps that had found their way down inside his coat, David put out a tentative hand. The slanting wall was made of canvas; it was a tent braced up against a rock. David threw great handfuls of snow into the air, hunting for the buried flap that would give him entrance.

All at once, he found it, and he flung himself into the dark embrace of the tent's interior.

Inside, he explored the corners and folds of canvas, coming up with a wrapped parcel. He tore it open. Pieces of hardtack biscuit flew all over the lean-to, and David eagerly pursued and devoured every one.

While he was crunching the bread, the snow abruptly ceased. When David emerged from the shelter, he knew with a sudden clarity where he was: he had come full circle to the giant rock from which he had been shot. Below him, far down the slope, he could just make out the lights of The Forks.

Christmas Eve. The snow lay deep around the settlement. Blue smoke from two hundred fires and stoves curled lazily upward in the early evening sky.

The tracks of three hundred homesick gold hunters led straight to the door of a stout log building on the edge of town. Native Hawaiians and Chinese coolies mingled with men from England and Maine and Virginia and Missouri. This evening there seemed to be no notice of race or accent. Men from every place on the globe turned their faces toward a memory of home, a vision of family.

With one yearning heart they trudged through the snow toward the newly constructed church of Pastor Kapono Bollin. The Reverend had pitched his tent and staked his claim at The Forks. It was the last place his son had been alive; here he would live and preach and wait for spring thaw when he could begin the search for his son's body once again.

The miners talked about it over bad whiskey in the

saloon. It was a sad story, the kind of story that made them think about their own fathers. A few even made the connection between some nearly forgotten Bible school story and the gold rush prodigal, David Bollin. In the original story the prodigal son had come home. But David Bollin was long dead. He would not be coming home.

Still, as men tramped up the steps of the new log church, they could not help but notice the way Pastor Bollin shook their hands and looked away up into the Sierras as if he were looking for someone else. Perhaps he was remembering some long-ago Christmas. Maybe he was seeing his boy opening a present or singing a Christmas carol. Ah, well. This was a hard winter. A hard Christmas for everyone in the Sierras. And this little church was as close to home as anyone was going to get.

The night lay in perfect stillness. Tiny crystals of snow drifted down from the pine boughs above David. His breath rose in a labored, steamy vapor from his cracked lips and then froze into icicles on his beard.

His legs continued to move mechanically, lifting first one foot forward and then the next. Always he stumbled toward the lights in the valley. The Forks. A town with people. Warmth. Food. He had long since stopped thinking of the gallows that awaited him. He had lived and died a hundred times since he had fled from his captors. To eat and sleep and be warm for the first time in weeks! To hold a pen in his hand and write his father a loving farewell, a plea for forgiveness for the grief he had brought on him! Death at the end of a hangman's rope seemed a small price to pay.

David stumbled and fell, tumbling headlong into a drift that covered him completely. A weight pressed down on him, a weariness that urged him to sleep a while. *Sleep tonight. Stay here. You can walk better in the daylight.*

He felt strangely warmed. His leg did not throb. He could almost feel his father's hands tucking him in to bed. And there! Behind him in the doorway . . .

"Mother?" David cried with a start, and the image evaporated. Suddenly he knew. He could not sleep, or he would never awaken again.

He forced his eyes open and struggled against the comfortable pull of death. The snow bound him, but he kicked up, searching for the cloudless, star-flecked sky through the treetops. An inch at a time he freed himself from the drift.

Managing to stand at last, he reached out to the trunk of a tree and leaned against it as he tried to clear his mind. Which way to go? The fall had muddled his sense of direction. To walk even a short distance the wrong way was as much a threat as if he lay down in the snow and did not rise. His strength was failing.

He raised his head and inhaled deeply. *Woodsmoke!* But where was it coming from?

Leaning his back against the tree, he sniffed again. The scent of smoke was strong before him. He circled halfway around the tree and drew another breath. On this side he could not smell the smoke.

Moving back to the front of the tree trunk, he fixed his senses on the smell of cooking fires. He moved from tree to tree, pulling himself through drifts that threatened to swallow him whole until spring thaw.

He did not want to die. Not yet. Not this way. The

face of his father loomed before him, urging him on. He imagined the warm kona winds blowing over his island home. It must be nearly Christmas. The people of the village would be gathered in the little white frame church. They would be praying for him.

"Yes!" he cried out to the silent forest. "Pray for me!" He stumbled forward to the next tree trunk and the next. In his mind he could hear the sweet strains of mellow voices singing:

Silent night, Holy night!
All is calm, All is bright!

The voices drifted on the cold wind. Like the wood smoke, the music drew him ever forward, one hard step at a time. *To falter was to die!*

Suddenly the music stopped. David clung to a tree and cried out, "Please! *Please!* I am lost! Please don't stop singing! Sobs half-choked him, and his knees began to give way to the weeks of starvation and the days of walking. Still his arms held him up. Encircling the rough bark of an oak, he kept himself from falling for the last time.

"Please," he whispered, "pray for me, Father. Mary. Edward . . . please. I'm right here. Here. I want to go . . ."

His words trailed off as once again he heard a faint refrain through the trees. He fought to quiet his labored breath. To hear words distinctly . . .

Could it be?

Once again the melody of *Silent Night* was clear. But now the faint words came to him in a familiar and dear tongue. Was he dreaming, or simply dying with one last sweet memory of home playing out in his fuddled brain? "*Silent night . . . ,*" the voices called. The refrain was followed by an answer in Hawaiian. "*Pola'i e, Pokamah-a'o . . .*"

David stretched out his hands toward the voices as if they could hold him up; pull him safely home. He stumbled forward, crying out the words he had sung every Christmas since he was a child.

His words slipped from English to Hawaiian. "*All is calm! All is bright! Ka makua-hi-aloha. . . .*"

He stumbled and fell, rose, and pitched forward again. Once more he fought to rise, to move toward the music. To move nearer toward home.

————

David coughed and brushed the snow from his face. His legs had failed him. He lay at the edge of the forest. A clearing opened up just beyond him. He could see lights twinkling below like bright warm stars. The drifts of snow around buildings glowed golden.

Men, bundled against the cold, walked toward a large log building. They opened the door, and light and warmth and music glowed out, then retreated as the door closed.

"*As close to home as a man can get,*" David muttered. Then he willed himself to rise again. He stood on the edge of the clearing and reached toward the building. It was a church. It was home—or at least as close to home as he would ever be again in this life.

Once more he moved toward the slope. He stumbled and slipped, rolling over and over down the hill. At the bottom, in a lane deep with mud and rutted with wagon tracks, David lay still for a moment, then sat up and measured the distance to the church.

The voices began to sing again, loud and bright: "*O come all ye faithful!*"

David stood swaying in the road. He pulled his shoulders erect and raised his chin as he took first one tentative step and then another. His thoughts flew toward home and all those who had loved him, those he now loved in return.

He would write. He would tell them. He would live long enough for that, at least. Nothing else seemed to matter as he staggered toward the church. He reached out to grasp the rough pole banister and pulled himself up the steps. The music was strong, filled with promise, hope, and joy!

David halted before the door and listened. Light seeped through the cracks and touched him. And now a clear, familiar voice resounded from the pulpit:

"Fear not: for behold, I bring you good tidings of great joy, which shall be to all the people!"

In those words, David Bollin heard the voice of his loving father. It was impossible, he knew. His father could not be in such a place as this. Yet his heart raced with joy as he groped toward the entrance.

In his mind he could see them all there. The pews crowded. Hands reaching heavenward and swaying with the music. Smiling faces. The arms of his father reaching out. He was home again! Home!

"Thank you, Father," he whispered. *"I've come home!"*

Then he opened the door and entered.

PO LA'I E
Silent Night, Holy Night

Joseph Mohr, 1792-1848
Eng. Tr. John F. Young, 1820-1885
Haw'n Tr. Stephen Desha

STILLE NACHT Irregular
Franz Gruber, 1787-1863

1. Po — la'i e, Po — kama-ha'o, Ma — lu — hia,
   Mālama-lama, Ka makuahine a — lo — ha, e,
   Me ke keiki He-mo-lele e, Moe me ka ma-lu-hia
   la — ni, Moe me ka ma-lu-hia la-ni.

2. Po — la'i e, Po — kama-ha'o, O — ni na Kahu-
   hi — pa e, I ko ka la — ni, na — ni no,
   Me le na a-ne-la Ha-le-lu-ia, Ha-nau ia Kris-to ka
   Ha-ku, Ha-nau ia Kris-to ka Ha-ku.

3. Po — la'i e, Po — kama-ha'o, Kei-ki hiwa-hi-wa a-
   lo-ha e, Ka la-ma la-'i mai lu-na mai,
   Me ka loko-ma-i-ka'i ma-ka-mae, Ie-su i kou ha-nau
   a-na, Ie-su i kou ha-nau a-na. A-mene.

"Silent Night, Holy Night" Hawaiian translation from *Na Himeni Haipule Hawaii*, © 1972 by Hawaii Conference, United Church of Christ. Used by permission.